ON A DISTANT SUN

ON A DISTANT SUN

A Novel

R.C. CUNNINGHAM

First published in 2020 by Milton Books

This edition published in 2020 by Milton Books

Milton Books
an imprint of Milton Books Limited
Acre House, 11/15 William Road,
London, United Kingdom,
NW1 3ER
www.booksmilton.com

Copyright © 2020 Milton Books Limited

The right of R.C. Cunningham to be identified
as the author of the work has been asserted by him

All rights reserved. No part of this publication may be reproduced in any
form or by any electronic or mechanical means, including information
storage and retrieval systems, without written permission from both the
publisher and copyright owner, except for the use of brief quotations in a
book review. For more information, please contact the publisher

This is a work of fiction. Names, characters, places, and incidents either are
the product of the author's imagination or are used fictitiously. Any
resemblance to actual persons, living or dead, events, or locales is entirely
coincidental

ISBN: 978-1-8380665-0-5 (paperback)
ISBN: 978-1-8380665-1-2 (ebook)

British Library Cataloguing-in-Publication Data
A catalogue record for this book is available from the British Library

Cover illustration/design by Andy Bridge

For anyone who ever had a story to tell.

Man conquers the world by conquering himself.

— ZENO OF CITIUM

PROLOGUE

After five nights on the mountain the traveler came down, weary and pensive, and found a cold stream in the dayspring meadow to wash himself.

He had traveled far to find the wise man that had shown him his ways and now left a changed man himself: no longer the same person he recognized in his reflection on the water as he bathed.

From there he picked up the broken trail towards the nearest town where he had left his trusty old steed, and when he arrived, he found a weather-worn bench in a quiet spot by the glistering lake and sat in the glaring light of high noon.

In the serene shade of warm waters he watched a school of bluegill come up to feed on the surface bugs, and he thought to himself what a perfect place to fish one day. And in his hand he held a silver coin—plain and featureless on both sides—which he rolled between his fingers. It was the last thing the wise man had given him before he had vanished; a token, he said, which he must keep with him always.

Before long he saw the old woman approaching, and she smiled as though she had been expecting him.

The traveler had happened upon the old woman on his first day in town, in much the same spot, and she had greeted him like the stranger he was, and with the same cordial smile that she approached with now. She walked weak-kneed and with a cane in one hand and carried a loaf of bread in the other with which to feed the greedy bluegill.

She came and sat beside him on the bench and tossed a fistful of breadcrumbs into the shallow waters. "You are back . . ." she said.

The traveler turned to her and grinned.

"And did you find what you were looking for?" she asked.

The traveler lifted his face to the sun and said, "More than I ever imagined."

They sat and watched the fish for a moment, bobbing on the surface, then the old woman reached into her pocket and took out a silver coin—plain and featureless and much like the traveler's own.

The traveler stared down at the old woman's coin, his mouth agape. "You have seen him too?" he said.

"Many moons ago now," she replied. "But I remember it as if it were yesterday."

The traveler opened his palm and showed the old woman his own coin.

"You must do as he said and keep it with you always," she continued. "For it is your guiding light in the darker days that may follow."

The traveler gazed down at his coin, then slipped it back into his pocket. "Do you know of anyone else?" he asked.

"Who has seen him like you and I?"

"Yes."

"There are plenty out there," she said, "living their lives;

no longer in the shadows. But there are many others who still live in doubt and do not believe he exists."

The traveler sighed, and they sat in silence for a long moment as the woman threw another fistful of bread for the bluegills to feast upon. "Do you have it with you?" she asked. "The map?"

The traveler nodded and removed a fold of paper from his jacket pocket. It was old and frayed and carried the marks of a hundred men and more. "What should I do with it?" he asked.

"You are the bearer of wisdom," she said. "A messenger of lore. But this is not for you alone, but to share with one man more."

The traveler held the map out in his hand. "Then who should I give to?"

"To someone much like yourself before today. Someone lost in the darkness. It is your duty." The old woman reached for her cane and stood. "I trust we may meet again some day," she said, and wandered off down the path from which she came.

CHAPTER 1

My feet were numb and restless, and I was in the sort of mood you found yourself in after a shift spent clock-watching and cleaning floors. The clock on the wall read 7:59 p.m., and still two more hours standing between this place and freedom.

The diner was empty, save for the young couple sat alone in the corner booth exchanging awkward glances over their vanilla milkshakes. First-daters.

I'd spent the last forty-five minutes spying on them from behind the counter, humming along to the rock-and-roll numbers playing on the jukebox. They were the only thing for company whilst Donny busied himself with paperwork in the back office behind closed blinds.

The rain was coming down in sheets outside, and the usual mid-week circus was nowhere to be seen; nobody was of a mind to venture out to a burger joint in this squall.

Donny's All-night Diner was about the only place worth frequenting in town. Any other Wednesday and the place would be full with folk from all over town—something which I had got used to managing single-handedly as Donny was too much of a miser to hire a second pair of hands to help—but the last few weeks had been a struggle. Something had changed.

I leaned across the formica counter, my heavy eyes begging for sleep as I rested my chin in my palm, and I heard the seconds ticking on the clock behind me. A moment later and the diner doors swung open, and Mitch Green and his mob of misfits walked in and shook down their wet coats on the tiled floor.

He came up to the counter and smirked. "Never get tired of seeing you in that fine hat, Driscoll," he said, referring to my red and white soda jerk hat, complete with a smiling burger face on the side and apron to match.

"What do you want, Mitch?" I said, with a deadpan expression. After six months, the uniform gibes had grown as old as his slicked-back quiff.

"Say it . . ." he replied.

"Excuse me?"

"C'mon, Driscoll, is this how you greet a loyal customer?"

I looked over his shoulder and caught sight of Rory and Stan approaching now. They were Mitch's bootlickers in every sense of the word. Wherever Mitch walked, Rory and Stan were only two steps behind. And behind them stood two girls that I didn't recognize, and another one I did: Jolie Green.

"Hey, Driscoll," Mitch said, clicking his fingers in my face. "I'm talking to you."

I ignored him, catching Jolie's eye as she came up to the counter and stood to Mitch's left.

"Hi, Hugo," she said, her smile as bright as the moon in a black sky.

"Hey, Jolie."

Ten years ago, Jolie and I had been as thick as thieves. Inseparable, some might say. She had been my first friend, and the only one I ever needed back then. But times change, and so do people, it seems. She was no longer the person I used to climb trees and ride bikes with, and we'd gone our separate ways as we'd grown older. But even though we didn't talk much these days, the fondness never left. History was funny like that.

"How are you?" she said.

I nodded. "I saw your mom the other day. She said she put the house up for sale and that your—"

Mitch knocked on the counter with his knuckles. "Sorry to interrupt this little trip down memory lane, but we're famished here, Driscoll."

I glared at him, and he was looking back at me with that same stupid smirk on his face.

"You were about to say something . . ." he said.

Mitch was trying to find another opportunity to embarrass me in front of Jolie. I knew what he wanted me to say, and so did she.

"Leave it alone, Mitch," Jolie said, putting a hand on his shoulder.

"No," he said, turning back to me again. "I want to hear him say it."

"Yeah, Driscoll, *say it*," Rory said, snorting and baring his buck teeth.

All of them stood and eyeballed me now. Even the lovebirds in the corner booth had turned to see the commotion.

Jolie looked off my stare and down at the floor.

I lifted my head, feigned a wide smile, and spoke with the gusto of a car salesman on a television commercial. "*Every day's a Donny's day!* May I take your order, please?"

A collective snicker went up, except for Mitch, who just looked me dead in the eye as he put an arm round Jolie and pulled her close to his side. She belonged to him, and he took pleasure in reminding me of that.

"I'll have the Donny Daddy with chillies and fries," Mitch said, turning to Jolie now. "And she'll have the Donny Delicious."

I turned to Jolie, and she gave a nod as Mitch laid down the money on the counter. I took the other orders and cashed up with a hangdog look on my face.

"Bring it over to us, Driscoll. We'll sit over there." Mitch winked, then found a table in the corner and sat with the others, leaving Jolie at the counter.

"Sorry," she said, struggling to look me in the eye.

"Forget about it," I said. "I heard you got the grades you needed. That's brilliant news."

She nodded. "Looks like the long nights reading books *does* actually work . . . for some of us."

I gave a mock smile, gathered up a tray and napkins for the table and said, "Yeah, I guess . . ."

I'd failed to get the grades I needed for a place at law school, which was my parents' favorite dinner topic of choice at the moment, much to their displeasure. I never wanted to go to law school, but my parents had a funny way of convincing me that every decision I made was the wrong one, so I ended up applying in the hope it would get them off my back, at least for the meantime.

A silence hung in the air like the suspended moment before a falling glass strikes the ground, and then Jolie creased up her face as the realization of what she had said dawned on her. "Oh, I . . . I didn't mean . . ." she said, the words stuck in her throat.

"It's fine," I said, "turns out I didn't want to study law as much as I thought I did."

"So what are your plans?"

"I'm still working that one out."

Jolie sighed and nodded again, and I wasn't sure if it was her tactless—though unintentional—blunder, or the obvious disappointment on her face, which had left a sudden bitter taste in my mouth.

"When do you leave?" I said.

"Three weeks." She turned as a paper pellet hit her on the side of the temple, then shot a look at Mitch, who sat there with a straw in his mouth and the wrapper rolled up into firing balls on the table.

"In your own time, Driscoll . . ." Mitch said.

Jolie turned back to me. "I better join the others."

"Sure," I said, "I'll bring it over in a minute."

"Maybe we can catch up before I leave. For old time's sake?"

All I could do was smile. "I'd like that."

She smiled back and joined the others at the table.

I was proud of Jolie. She never had been the academic-type. In fact, I had always been the bookworm growing up, educating her on everything from black holes to biology. She, well, she liked everything else other than books, but always made time to listen to me. That's how I remember Jolie: she was the listener, and I was the talker. Like I said before, times change.

Mitch ignored me when I took the food over to the table, and I returned to my spot at the counter and watched Jolie from a distance as she talked and laughed with her new cronies. She appeared unfamiliar to me these days; no longer the shy kid playing in the dirt, but a woman. And a beautiful one at that. But even behind this changed image of hers, I could still see the old Jolie. Somewhere in there. She'd never lost that.

I loved her, but it was a unique love. A platonic love. A fondness. It wasn't the same love I had for Sarah.

Sarah had always been around, for as long as I could remember, but it wasn't until the party at Jesse Cole's place last October that I ever really *looked* at her. We'd grown up in the same year at school, but she had always been the quiet one who kept company with kids that dyed their hair purple and painted their nails black. But when she turned up that night at Jesse's house, all alone and without a friend in the world, I felt an urge in my stomach. So I just walked up to her and started talking. In fact, we spent the entire night talking and drinking, and it was like one of those strange moments when you realize you share more in common with your opposite number than you ever imagined. Pete and the gang left me to it, thinking I'd lost a screw or something, but it was a night that I knew would stay with me for a long time. Sometimes you just get that feeling.

It turned out that Sarah's so-called friends weren't even going to Jesse's party that night, they'd just forgotten to tell her. It was a lie, and she knew it. But I was grateful for it, and I think she was too.

MITCH and the gang left soon after they'd finished their burgers, and I got back to reading Hemingway's *The Old Man and the Sea*, which I kept hidden under the counter for the quiet nights and idle hours when Donny wasn't watching. Come to think of it, I hadn't really seen much of Donny these days. In the past month he'd taken to his office as soon as I started my shift and kept the blinds closed until I had finished. I thought he had been trying to avoid me at first, but then I had noticed that he'd been losing weight. And on the rare occasions he emerged from his hole, he was always sighing and rubbing his neck like he had mites. In fact, I was sure he'd been wearing the same clothes for the last week, and from the black rings under his eyes, I'd wager he wasn't getting any more than a few hours' shut-eye each night.

Donny was struggling, that much was clear. He never said

why, but I had seen a few letters on his desk from the bank when he'd left the door unlocked, each one stamped with a red notice. I never said a word to him about it; he was a proud man. But he had not been himself of late.

THE TRAVELER CAME in twenty minutes before the end of my shift, just as I was finishing the last page of my book. He had blonde hair and a ruddy face and wore his plaid shirt with three buttons open at the chest. To anyone who didn't know any better, he looked like a wild wayfarer who'd taken a wrong turn into town.

"Good evening," I said. "Welcome to Donny's."

He walked over to the counter, squinted against the harshness of the strip lights, and sat down on the stool at the counter. "Busy night?" he said, looking about the empty booths.

"Rushed off my feet," I said, raising a brow. "Can I get you anything?"

The traveler looked up at the menu displayed overhead. "Just a water, if it's not too much trouble."

"You want anything else with that?"

"Maybe a glass," he said. "And some ice."

I looked at him for a moment, expecting more, but he just eyeballed me and smiled. I grabbed a bottle from the fridge, a clean glass from the shelf, and poured the water over three cubes of ice.

The traveler gulped the cold water down in one and said, "What did you think of it?"

I glanced up at him with narrowed eyes and said, "Excuse me?"

He pointed to the copy of *The Old Man and the Sea*, which

I had placed to one side of the counter. "The book," he said. "What did you think?"

The book had belonged to my grandfather once, and had been one of his favorites, but I had never gotten around to reading it until now.

It told the story of an old fisherman who, after eighty-four days without a catch, heads out into deeper seas where he battles to hook a giant marlin; the greatest catch of his entire life. Unable to pull the fish in, or tie the line to his skiff, the fisherman holds onto the line with his bare hands for two days and two nights, enduring the agony that entails. On the third day, the fish grows weary, and the fisherman, dog-tired and sore himself, fights to pull the fish in close enough to kill it with a harpoon. After lashing the marlin to his boat, the fisherman heads home with his prize. But along the way, the marlin's blood leaves a trail in the water, and the fisherman struggles to fight off the ravenous sharks, which reduce the fish to nothing more than a carcass. So the old man returns home the same as he left: empty-handed.

"I think he should have thrown the fish back and just moved on," I said.

The traveler smiled. "Then you should try reading it again."

"Why's that?"

"Because you missed the point." He topped up his water from the bottle and leaned back.

"And what *is* the point?" I said.

"The fisherman did not give up on the fish because, despite the many challenges he faced in catching it, his spirit remained undefeated, even when he returned home with nothing but his boat. Because no man is made for defeat in this world. *That* is the point."

I nodded and said, "I'll bear that in mind."

He smiled again. "Are you Donny?"

"No," I said. "He's back there." I pointed to the office behind me, the blinds still down. "You want me to get him for you?"

The traveler shook his head and studied me for a moment. On the surface he didn't seem threatening, but there was something peculiar about him.

"You like it here?" he said.

I gave him the courtesy of a considered response. "It pays okay."

"I didn't ask if it pays okay," he said. "I asked if you liked it here . . ." His tone was more curious than condescending.

"You mean the job?"

"The job. This town. Whatever."

The question caught me off guard. It was odd.

Had Donny put him up to this? To test my loyalty?

"It's human nature to want something . . . different. Right?" I said.

"A fool might say so."

We exchanged awkward glances.

Was he calling me a fool?

"If you're not happy, then you can change whatever's going on in your life," he continued. "You know that?"

"We'd have to agree to disagree on that," I replied.

There was another silence between us.

"I used to be like you," he said. "I was for a long time."

Here we go, I thought to myself, another guy waxing philosophical right before the end of my shift. Donny's had a strange way of attracting these kinds of traveling folk, and I'd listened to this story before, except on a different night and from a different mouth.

"Is that so?" I said, rolling my eyes as I wiped down the counter.

The traveler cleared his throat and sipped on his water this time. "I've done some things in my life I'm not so proud of," he said. "But there's only one thing I really regret."

"What's that?" I said, checking the clock on the wall.

"Being sorry about the things I had no control over."

I nodded politely.

"I know what you're thinking: who's this fruitcake coming in here lecturing me about life . . ." he said. "Am I right?"

"I wasn't thinking that," I said, but my eyes betrayed my confidence.

The traveler smiled again. "I'm on my way home to see my little girl," he said. "I've got some things I need to put right."

"Well, I hope you work things out." I was paying the man lip service, no doubt about it. Donny didn't pay me enough to stand here and listen to people's woes over a glass of water.

"We've all got our own adventure to live, kid," he said. "And we've all got to take control of it."

"I guess so," I said, scratching my head and wishing this guy would leave already.

"You ever heard of the wise man who lives on the mountain?" he said.

I glanced up at the clock again and stretched my back. "Is it another book?"

The traveler laughed. "No," he said, "he's real. Some say he's an urban legend. Others say he's three hundred years old. I don't know if that's true, but he's no legend."

"How so?"

"I've met him."

I gave a half-nod and went back to cleaning the counter. "Uh huh," I replied.

"Look, I understand if you don't believe me," he said. "But it's true. And he changed my life."

We stood looking at one another for a long moment.

"Listen, I don't mean to be rude," I said, "but I've got to finish cleaning the tables before the end of my shift."

The traveler cast a glance over his shoulder at the spotless booths and tabletops. "Okay," he said, pursing his lips. "You do what you got to do, kid. Can I use your restroom?"

"It's right over there," I said, pointing to a door at the far left corner of the diner.

The traveler got to his feet. "Thanks."

By the time he'd returned, I'd worked my way round to the farthest booth in the diner and did my best to avoid eye contact. From the reflection in the mirror, hanging above the counter, I saw the traveler down the rest of his water and start for the door.

"Thanks for the refuel, kid," he said, as he threw on his jacket and stepped outside. "And good luck."

I smiled and finished up in the corner booth and checked the clock again. As I crossed the floor of the diner, I spotted something atop the counter. At first it looked like a folded newspaper, but as I got nearer, I could see it was something else: a map.

I grabbed it off the top, turned on my heel, and ran for the door, but the traveler was already on his motorcycle as I heard the engine roar to life. And by the time I stepped out into the parking lot, he was burning rubber down the highway into the black of the night.

I stood and waited for a moment, expecting him to turn back. But he never did.

The rain had stopped falling now, which meant I could walk the two miles home without getting soaked to the bone. I slipped the map into my back pocket as I stepped back into the diner, and saw Donny watching me from behind the counter.

"I don't pay you to be anywhere else but inside these four

walls," he said, a wretched look in his eye. He was unshaven, and his skin was pallid and drawn.

"Sorry, Donny," I said.

"In fact," he said. "I won't be able to pay you anymore after tonight."

I creased up my face, confused. "What do you mean?"

Donny came over to me and handed me a manila envelope with my wages in, just like he did at the end of every week. But this was Wednesday.

"This will be the last paycheck," he said, his eyes heavy and dark-circled. He looked terrible.

I glanced up at him and said, "If it's about—"

"I'm not letting you go," he said. "I've got to close the place down." His head was low about his chest, unable to face me. "I wish I could say more but, the truth is, I can't afford to keep it going any longer."

I shook my head in disbelief. "Donny—"

"No questions, Hugo. Just take your paycheck and go home."

"But I need this job."

"I'll give you a reference. Best I can offer."

"Donny, please?"

"Go home."

I took off my soda jerk hat and apron, placed them on the side, and left.

I'D MADE the walk home many times before, but this time it felt so final. It *was* final.

The moon was up and the rain had passed, and all I could think about was calling Sarah. I tried her on the cellphone ten times before giving up. Sarah had texted me earlier to say she was busy tonight, but wanted to meet tomorrow to talk about something. I guessed it would be something to do with her parents' divorce; I had never pressed her on the subject, but figured she'd just tell me what I needed to know when the time was right.

The two miles back into town gave me some welcome space to clear my head, but I stopped by Sarah's on the way, despite her message. I wasn't ready to face my parents' disappointment just yet, and she was the only person I could speak to. The only person who would understand.

By the time I'd made it to Sarah's street, the rain had started up again, and I saw the lights on inside in her house and her mother's car missing from the drive. In fact, there was another car parked up outside her house I hadn't seen before.

I wiped my hair away from my face, and the door opened as I approached the front steps, and a tall guy in a hoodie stepped out. I couldn't see his face, but I saw a flash of Sarah's red hair over his shoulder, and then the side of her face as he turned to her.

She smiled at him and played with her hair, then leaned in to kiss him.

I could feel my heart in my throat, and my eyes went wide as I stepped down off the bottom step.

They pulled back from one another as the sound of my foot hit the sidewalk, and Sarah opened her eyes and saw me standing there, looking up at her.

She pushed the guy in the hoodie to one side, and I watched all the blood drain from her face.

"Hugo . . ." she said. "What are you doing—"

Before she could finish, I was on my toes and running.

CHAPTER 2

I ran until I made it home. My face was damp with sweat as I climbed the front steps, and I could feel my heart exploding in my chest. For a moment, I stood in the warm breeze to catch my breath, and patted my brow dry with the back of my shirt sleeve.

The night was hot and sticky, and pools of rainfall had gathered by the curbside. I took another deep breath and listened to the thrumming of cicadas in the trees.

My house was one of a row of many others on a tree-lined street in little suburbia. A quiet road where neighbors got along and enjoyed Sunday mornings manicuring their lawns and polishing their cars as they exchanged pleasantries over garden fences. It had always been that way.

I sat down on the wicker chair on the porch and gathered my thoughts. There were tears in my eyes, but I stifled a sob. I didn't want my parents to see me like this. For a moment, it occurred to me that I might have imagined everything, or at least misjudged what I had seen.

Did they really kiss? Was that definitely Sarah?

The scene played over and over in my head and, as much

as I wanted to believe I was wrong, the better part of me knew my mind wasn't playing tricks.

She kissed him. Whoever *he* was.

I checked my cell as I stepped through the front door, and a string of missed calls flashed up on the screen. All from Sarah. I switched it off and slipped it back into my pocket.

The lights were on in the living room as I came through the hall and kicked off my sodden shoes and threw my coat on the rack. At this hour, my father would be asleep in front of the television with his feet up on his well-worn stool, and my mother would be next to him reading, if she hadn't already turned in for the night.

I closed the front door, being as quiet as possible, and tiptoed down the hall towards the stairs.

My father's voice called out as I reached the bottom step. "How was your shift?" he said. He was awake.

I moseyed into the living room to see my father sat upright in his wingback chair, watching an old war film on the television, and my mother glanced up behind the frayed corners of her book.

"Slow night. Same as always," I said.

"There's leftover stew in the oven if you want some?" my mother said.

"I already ate."

"If you're sure, Hon," she said, pushing her glasses back onto her face. She stared at me for a moment, then said, "Is everything else okay?"

Perhaps it was maternal instinct kicking in, but she must have seen the puffiness in my eyes and the redness in my skin to realize something wasn't right. Still, I had no intention of having a heart-to-heart about anything.

"Everything's fine, Mom," I said. "I'm going to bed."

She lifted a brow and smiled. "Okay, Hon. See you in the morning."

I took to my bedroom as quick as my jellied-legs could carry me, and before my father uttered another word.

Watching my parents had become too much to bear in recent years. Most of the time they filled their days doing their own thing, coming together only for the ritual family supper, which comprised small-talk and painful silence.

It wasn't their fault. They had grown apart over the past few years, but only now was it so apparent. They spoke to each other only when they had to, and that was that; what remained of any affection between them went unseen. But they didn't like to talk about it, and they did their best to carry on as if it wasn't even a thing. They only stayed together for Elijah, my brother; my mother had confessed as much one night when my father came home full of whisky and with nowhere else to go, which was not an infrequent occurrence. She meant it, too, but I guessed the feeling was mutual for my father.

They never fought. I couldn't remember a time when they ever had. But perhaps that was their problem. They avoided confrontation and refused to settle their differences. And when you live in a house with twenty years of unsettled differences, you won't find a happy home, only the imitation of one for those looking in.

As I pulled off my wet clothes, there was a knock on my bedroom door. I threw on a clean shirt and some pants and saw Elijah come in. "You should be asleep," I said.

He rubbed his eyes and yawned and stood there in his pajamas. He was short for his eight years, just like I had been, but he was my best friend in this world.

"Can I come in?" he said.

"You already are," I replied, unpacking my rucksack onto the bed. "Best make it quick. You don't want Dad catching you out of bed at this hour."

Elijah shuffled into my room and closed the door behind him. "Can we play Nintendo?" he said.

"Not now, El, it's late. Maybe tomorrow."

He said nothing, just watched me for a moment.

"Have you been crying?" he said.

"No," I said, turning away from his stare. "It's just the rain."

Elijah walked over to the window and looked outside. "It's not raining," he said.

"It was."

"I'm not stupid. I know you've been crying."

Stupid he wasn't and curse me for ever assuming I was smarter than him.

"It's been a long day," I replied.

"You can talk to me," he said. "I'm a good listener." He stood there like a soldier on guard, waiting patiently.

I sighed. "When you're older, you'll understand that life is nothing but a massive disappointment."

He screwed up his face. "How come?"

"Like I said, one day you will understand. For now, you just worry about going back to bed."

Elijah came over and sat next to me. "What're you reading?" he said.

He was looking down at my grandfather's copy of *The Old Man and the Sea*.

"It's about a guy trying to catch a big fish." I said.

"You're reading a book about a fish?" he replied, as he picked it up.

I rolled my eyes. "It's about a man trying to catch a fish."

"And does he?"

"Read it and find out for yourself."

"It looks old."

"It *is* old," I said. "It belonged to Grandpa."

He looked at it for a moment, then put it back down on the bed.

"What do you want to do when you grow up?" I said.

"Like a job?"

"It can be anything."

"An astronaut," he said, beaming. "You already know that."

"Still?"

"Why not?" he replied, shrugging his shoulders. "Or a truck driver."

"An astronaut or a truck driver . . ." I said, raising a brow. "They're very different."

"Not really," he replied.

"How so?"

"Truck drivers explore the world. Astronauts explore the universe."

"So what you really want to be is an explorer?"

He took a moment to muse on it and said, "I guess so."

"Sounds lonely."

"I don't mind," he said. "What are *you* going to do?"

"About what?"

"About the reason you're upset . . ."

"I'm not upset."

"Sure," he said.

"Let's just say I'm trying to figure things out."

Elijah got to his knees and reached a hand under my bed. "I got you something," he said, passing me a notebook bound in a green leather cover with a gold *H* embossed on the front. "I saw it in the shop down the road."

"You bought this for me?"

"You're always writing," he said. "I figured you could write in this."

"Thank you, El. It's perfect."

"Maybe one day you'll write a video game," he said, smiling his toothy smile.

"Maybe," I said, as I set the notebook down beside me. "But now it's time to go to bed."

Elijah hugged me, then started for the door.

"El?" I said, and he turned to face me. "Don't come into my room on your own again."

"Not even to hide something?"

"Especially not that."

Elijah smiled and pulled a face. I made one back.

He closed the door behind him, and I fell back onto my bed and let my head hit the pillow. I lolled there for a moment and closed my eyes and thought about Mitch and Jolie and Donny and Sarah. Someone once said that bad things come in threes. By my calculation, I had exhausted my quota of ill fortune for a while, so tomorrow had to be a better day.

As I turned on my side, I saw something sticking out of the back pocket of my jeans crumpled on the floor: it was the map the traveler had left at the diner.

I reached a hand down and unfolded it, being careful not to tear the worn edges, and studied it for a long while. I didn't recognize any landmarks on the map as being local, but as I moved my eyes from left to right across the page, I could make out a mountain range, and at the foot of the mountain, there was a drawing of what appeared to be a small town. And at the bottom of the map it read:

Mount Cato

Hadn't the traveler mentioned something about a mountain, and some old, wise man who lived on one?

The story sounded like bunkum, but maybe there *was* something to this map.

What if the traveler had left the map behind on purpose? What if it was a sign? Had he seen all this coming? Was he a messenger? An oracle? He was strange, and that was all I knew.

There were too many questions that I couldn't answer, but, for the first time, I felt a sense of urgency. A calling of sorts. The map was speaking to me somehow, but I didn't know how, or why.

All I knew is that I had to find out.

MY PARENTS WERE asleep in their chairs when I went back down. My father's mouth was hung open like a fly trap, as if waiting for its prey, and my mother's glasses had fallen off her face again and come to rest on the bridge of her nose.

As I stepped into the living room, the floorboards creaked under my feet, and my father stirred from his slumber, wiping the spittle away from the side of his mouth.

"Hugo . . ." he said, in a daze. "How long have you been standing there?"

"Not long," I replied.

"I thought you'd gone to bed?"

I stood over him as he adjusted himself in his chair. "I need to ask you something . . ."

He looked at me and yawned. "Well," he said, "what is it?"

"I'm going to stay with a friend out of town for a few days—"

My father raised a hand. "What friend? You don't have any friends out of town."

"I wanted to ask if I can borrow the car?"

My dad sat upright in his chair and almost choked. "Marcy?" he said, clearing his throat. "Marcy, are you hearing this?"

My mother stirred now and pushed her glasses back onto her nose.

"Did you hear that?" my father repeated.

My mother shook her head in dazed confusion. "Hear what?"

"Your son here wants to take the car out of town."

"It's just for a few days, that's all," I said.

My mother turned to look at me. "What for, Hon?"

"Seeing a friend, he says," my father replied.

My mother gazed at me, the cogs in her head spinning. "What friend?"

"That's what I said," my father replied, getting to his feet now.

"Just a friend," I said. "They moved to the city a while back."

"Who did?" she said.

"The whole family."

My mother pinched the corners of her eyes. "What about your job, Hon? Doesn't Donny need you at the diner?"

"He said I can take a few days off."

"Then have you thought more about what you want to do . . . with college and all?"

There it was again. If there was an opportunity to drag it up and slip it into conversation, my mother would find a way.

My father stretched his back and rubbed his chin. "He can come and work with me," he said. "My offer still stands."

"I don't want to sell cars."

"What's wrong with selling cars?" he replied. "Have you got anything else better to do right now?"

I didn't respond this time.

"I can teach you the trade. It's in the blood," he continued.

My father had learned everything about selling cars from his father, and his father before him; they were businessmen born and bred, and good at it too. But I had no inclination to follow in my father's footsteps.

"Then what about me?" my mother said.

"What about it?" I asked.

"I'm sure we can get you a few hours at the office for a bit of extra cash until something more . . . *permanent* comes along."

"I don't want to work—"

"He'll think about it," my father said. "If you don't want to work with me, then you'll go and work with your mother."

I rolled my eyes. "Fine. Can I please borrow the car now?"

"I don't think that's the best idea, Hon," my mother said.

My father looked at my mother with a strange glint in his eye and nodded. "Couldn't agree more."

It was the first time I had seen my parents agree on something for as long as I could remember. By the stunned silence, I think we must have all had the same thought.

"It's not the time to be skipping town," my father said, breaking the uncomfortable silence.

I held my mother's gaze, my eyes pleading with hers. She shrugged her shoulders and shook her head.

Realizing this was going nowhere, I took to my bedroom again, and before I had made it up the stairs, I had already planned that I would take the bus tomorrow morning instead.

I squatted and reached for the shoe box under my bed and took every coin and note I could find in there, placed it into my wallet, then slid the wallet into my rucksack. It was all the savings I had to my name, but it was *mine*. And mine to do what I wanted with.

After that, I picked out a few clean shirts hanging up in the wardrobe, some underwear and socks from the drawer, and a spare pair of jeans to boot, and I'd made plans to raid the fridge in the morning for any other supplies before anyone else was up. Mom did the grocery shopping on

Friday's, but I'd have to make do with what scraps I could find.

Finally, I grabbed the notebook and slipped the map inside the front cover, put everything inside my rucksack, and laid back down on the bed. I checked my phone for messages, and there were no less than five from Sarah, but I couldn't bring myself to read them. And as I buried myself between the sheets, I heard the patter of rain against the window again.

CHAPTER 3

I was up at first light, before the rest of the world had woken.

My father was snoring, and I could hear Elijah talking in his sleep as I emerged from my room and made my way downstairs on gentle foot. I grabbed some supplies of bread and corned beef from the cupboard, and a two-day-old donut, which was on the turn.

I scrawled a note for my parents and left it on the table. I'd be back in a few days, it said, and I told them not to worry. But they'd still worry; it was a parents' prerogative.

It had often occurred to me that no matter how old you became, your parents will always view you as a child. I'm sure it was that way for most people.

Every family has their own dynamics, but the one thing they all have in common is that each person has their defined role. And a child is just that: a child. And it would remain that way until the child grows old enough to have a family of their own and pass off their parents' convictions and beliefs as though they were their own too. We are, after all, nothing but the echoes of our parents' teachings.

A small queue had already gathered by the ticket desk when I arrived at the bus stop. The clerk was perched behind a window, and the first buses of the day were pulling up outside. I joined the queue at the back and waited my turn.

"Destination?" the clerk said, without lifting his head as I approached the desk.

"I need to get to Mount Cato," I replied.

He peered up at me now. "Never heard of it," he said.

I pulled out the map from my rucksack and pressed it against the glass. "It's right here."

The clerk looked over the rim of his glasses and squinted. "Like I said before, I've never heard of it."

I folded the map and placed it back into my rucksack again, and the elderly couple behind me coughed and began whispering to one another.

"Where does the first bus go to?" I asked.

"Goes right through to Springfield," the clerk said.

"Okay," I said, "Can I get a ticket?"

∽

THE JOURNEY to Springfield was long and hot, and I slept for most of it, waking only for comfort breaks or to eat or to write in my notebook. I wrote about Donny and Sarah, and as we rode past golden fields and sea-green grasslands, I thought back to the traveler from the night before, and the old, wise man on the mountain he spoke of.

Three hundred years old. How was that even possible? No one had lived that long. But if anyone was to know anything about life, I figured it would be him.

The bus pulled over in the center of Springfield, one of many sleepy, single-street towns outside the city limits. The sun sat like an orange orb on the skyline as we disembarked outside a bookshop with a flaking wooden sign hanging from the stucco wall. I stretched my legs and arched my back and reached for the handle.

The bell dinged as I entered the store, and the smell of old books was overwhelming. The place was a storybook grotto of a bygone era, and, from the look of the proprietor slumbering in his chair to the trill of a fiddle playing on the radio, it was a place that enjoyed a slower pace of custom.

The proprietor stirred at the second ding of the bell as the door closed behind me, and I stood motionless for a moment, embarrassed at waking him.

He rubbed his face and reached for his glasses, which were hanging from a length of string around his neck. "That's not a face I recognize around here," he said. The proprietor had a bulbous nose and wore a pencil mustache that was graying at the ends. He got to his feet and wiped the rims of his glasses with a handkerchief which he retrieved from inside his sleeve, then narrowed his eyes as he inspected me again.

"I'm just passing through," I said.

"Like every other soul who comes in here it seems," he replied.

I moved through the shop towards the counter. "I'm looking for somewhere . . ." I said.

"Somewhere that ain't here I'm guessing?"

"Would you mind if I showed you something?" I said. "I thought you might be able to help."

"That depends."

"On what?"

"On whether or not you're a paying customer . . ."

I turned to the shelf nearest to my left and scanned the spines of the books on display. I reached for one, absent-mindedly, and carried it over to the counter.

"Excellent choice," the proprietor said.

I looked down at the cover of a bearded man sat on a

desert island with a musket in one hand and a parrot on his shoulder. The title of the book was *Robinson Crusoe*.

"What's this place you're looking for?" he continued.

I withdrew the map from my rucksack and spread it out on the countertop. "It's called Mount Cato."

The proprietor studied the map for a moment, then looked back up at me. "That'll be seven-fifty," he said.

Up close, his face was ashen and pitted, and he looked none too pleased by my inquiry, so I placed the money for the book on top, and returned the map to my rucksack.

After he cashed up, the proprietor put the book in a brown paper bag and handed it to me. "Word of advice: don't bother yourself with that mountain, or whatever it is you've been told is up there."

"You know where it is?" I said.

The proprietor let out a deep sigh. "Did you listen to what I just said? Don't go wasting your time up there."

"What do you know about it?"

"Enough to understand that too many men have wasted their time chasing folk tales, that's what."

"Have you been there?"

"No," he said, turning his nose up at me. "Why on earth would I?"

"So how do you *know*?"

The proprietor sighed and leveled with me. "Listen to me," he said, fixing me with a stare, "people come and go from that place all the time, but it's nothing but nonsense. There's no soul living up on that mountain. It's just a legend passed from person to person for a hundred years and more. So, save yourself the bother, and go back the way you came."

"But if you've never been, how can you be certain?"

He leaned across the counter and pursed his lips now. "Like I said before," he said, "you're wasting your time. But you've got that hell-bent look in your eye and I can see that nothing I will say to you will make a blind bit of difference, will it?"

I stood in silence and shook my head.

He eyeballed me and rolled his eyes. "You need to head for a place called Meridian. The town sits at the foot of the mountain, but it's remote."

"How do I get there?"

"It's about thirty miles west of here," he said, looking down at me now. "A long walk for fledgling legs."

I nodded and thanked him. "Is there anywhere around here I can get a room for the night?"

"You'll find a motel a mile or so down yonder," he said, pointing in a southerly direction. "Tell them Lou Carpenter sent you."

"Thank you," I replied, and I left as quick as my legs could carry me.

∼

THE MOTEL WAS easy to find, being the only one for miles on the single stretch of barren road south of Springfield. Three cars were parked in bays as I crossed the parking lot into the motel office: a vest-pocket building to the side that was separated from the guest rooms.

Four musicians in black t-shirts were busy loading instruments and equipment into the back of a waiting tour bus, and I noticed that one of them was carrying a custom 1963 Fender Stratocaster as he came towards me. It had a wine-red body and a black neck and pick guard; the slackness in my jaw must have given away my sudden fascination.

"Do you play?" the musician said.

"Yeah," I replied, "a little."

He handed me the Fender, and I gripped the neck tight in my palm.

"Cody Jones," he said, proffering a hand.

"Hugo Driscoll," I replied. We shook hands, and I admired the beauty of the guitar.

"You want to play her?" Cody said.

"Thanks," I said, passing the Fender back to him, "but I've got to check-in."

"No problem, man."

I turned on my heel and started for the motel office. Inside was a heavyset woman behind the check-in desk, doing a crossword and eating noodles from white cartons.

"It's thirty-five a night. Sixty for two," she said, her head buried in her food.

"Just need the one," I replied.

The woman set her chopsticks down, rose from her seat, and disappeared into the back room.

"So what brings you this way, Hugo Driscoll?"

I turned to the voice which came from behind me and saw Cody stood there.

"Just passing through," I said. "I'll be going east to Meridian tomorrow."

"Really?" Cody remarked. "We're going right by there. You can ride with us if you want?"

Over Cody's shoulder I could see the rest of the band had finished loading their stuff onto the back of the tour bus and were waiting to leave.

"Besides," he continued, leaning into my ear, "they don't wash the bedsheets in this place."

Cody squirmed, and I shuddered at the thought. At that moment the woman came back with a room key and placed it down on top.

"He won't be needing that anymore," Cody said.

"Huh?" the woman replied, and she stood there with a wrinkled forehead and noodle-juice around her mouth.

Cody placed another key down next to it and winked at

her. "We're checking out," he said. "Come on, man. Let's get out of here."

∽

FIVE MINUTES later and I was on the road again, in the tour bus to Meridian with Cody and his band. We passed the time talking music and drinking beer, and Cody told me of his plans to tour the entire country on this bus. So far, The Solomon's—that was the name of his band—had played in almost every major city on the east coast.

"West coast is the dream, my man," he said to me, swilling on a beer. "Better weather. Better women."

He laughed, passed me another bottle from the cooler, and popped the cap. "What's in Meridian anyway?" he said. "Have you got family there?"

"No, I'm looking for someone," I said.

"In Meridian?"

"Yeah."

"A girl?"

"Not exactly."

"It is, isn't it?" he said, nudging me in the shoulder. "Nice one, man!" Cody nodded and then held out his bottle of beer. "Well, good luck to that. Here's to new friends and new beginnings."

We chinked bottles to toast, and I sat back in my seat. "Do you like this life?" I said. "Traveling around. Playing music."

"Sure," Cody replied, "it has its trials, being away from home a lot, but I wouldn't want it any other way." Cody picked up another guitar and strummed some chords and sang a song. It was a gentle tune, and his voice carried the vestiges of true heartache. When he'd finished, he placed the guitar back down beside him and turned to me. "We all want to leave our mark on the world," he said. "A legacy. For some people it's money and fame. For others it's a child or a painting. For me, it will always be music. What about you?"

"I don't know. I guess I never really thought much about it."

"You'll figure it out, man. One day it will just come to you."

~

THE SUN WAS DOWN and the stars were up by the time Cody and The Solomon's had dropped me off in Meridian.

The town was a winsome sight at night, nestled in the foothills between two mountain ranges, and formed around its selfsame lake which was the heart of the community. Its cobbled streets were alive with music and fanfare when I arrived, and people were dancing and partying as if it were a nightly jamboree. And if you looked close enough, you could just make out the peak of Mount Cato rising in the land to the north.

The place was buzzing, and its energy was infectious. But with more than enough hours on the road for one day, I searched for the nearest place where I could rest my head for the night.

~

I FOUND Jerry's Inn on a corner of the main plaza, and the place was packed to the brim when I entered. The décor was like something out of an old western movie, with its batwing doors and wraparound bar, and there was a man playing the piano in the corner. Upstairs were several rooms for resting.

The bartender saw me approach the bar and came over,

cleaning a glass with a cloth. "What business you got here, kid?" he said.

"I was hoping I could get a bed for the night. Do you have one?"

"Uh huh," he replied, looking me up and down. "You're heading up that mountain, aren't you?"

"Wasn't planning on it."

He shot a look at the rucksack hanging from my shoulders. "You come in here wearing a pack on your back and I'd say you were lying."

"So what if I am?"

The bartender smiled. "You're not the first," he said. "And you won't be last. But you're wasting your time. There's no one up that mountain. I've lived here long enough to know."

I nodded politely. "Well," I said, "if it's all the same to you, I'd just like to get some rest."

"We've got a room upstairs. It's yours if you want it?"

∿

AFTER PAYING in cash I went straight to the room with a club sandwich and sat down to read *Robinson Crusoe* and his adventures at sea and on shipwrecked islands inhabited by cannibals. I read through the night until the sounds of music and merrymakers had ended, then rested my head on the cold pillow and shut my eyes.

CHAPTER 4

My eyes were bloodshot and dark-ringed when I woke the next morning. The bed was hard, and I had barely slept.

I took a cold shower to rouse my senses, got dressed, and followed the main road north out of town, using the wooden signs and the map to guide me, until I reached the foot of the mountain.

Mount Cato rose like the rugged spine of the land, and its granite peaks stood like ghostly sentries as they soared into the wild blue above. The range was higher to the east, and lower to the west, curling at the lip like a dragon's tail, and the foothills sat like rugs of green, yellow, and scarlet, from which rocky outcrops loomed like ancient obelisks. And beyond the alpine meadows, waterfalls cascaded like blankets of white lawn, and in the fields I could see the amber glint of Lake Meridian as the dayspring sun crested a hill.

I picked up the faint remnants of a path that twisted its way round sharp crags, and followed the trail of wild flowers as I climbed to the top of the ridge, stopping only to take in the sun-kissed vista below where Lake Meridian sat in all her beauty.

As I leveled off at the top, a golden eagle, perched on a small outcrop, turned its head as I approached; its yellow eyes watched my every move. As I moved closer, the bird took wing, and I stood to watch the eagle soar, then descend below the rock face.

There were no signs of other life as I continued along the ridge, just bluffs and more rocky outcrops.

∽

THE SUN WAS HIGH NOW, and I took in a sharp breath to savor the mountain air, and all I could think about was how stupid I had been. There was nothing living up here. There was no wise man. There was nothing at all.

I picked up a loose stone, threw it high across a deep ravine, and watched it sink towards the valley floor below. I never heard the sound as it hit the bottom. Yet I climbed, higher and higher still, until I caught sight of the soft wisps of white smoke rising from a plateau in the distance.

I followed the trail until the faint aroma of firewood filled my nose, and I saw a log cabin nestled amongst some trees, sheltered by a wall of jagged rock and set back from the cliff edge. There was a smaller barn right across from the cabin, and several chicken coops and runs scattered about the place.

My feet had swollen to twice their size and my legs were aching, but the smell of firewood, stronger now as I approached the cabin, made the pain worth bearing.

"Hello?" I said, but there was nothing but the echo of my voice across the mountain.

I called again, louder this time. "Hello?"

"No need to shout," came a voice from behind me.

"Sounds carry well in the wind up here, and there's no one else but me to hear them."

The voice was timeworn, yet had a mellowness to it. Before me stood a silver-haired man with folds on his face as deep as the mountain crevasses.

"Sorry," I said, as I looked off his stare.

The old man's beard covered his mouth, but it appeared he was smiling as his cheeks swelled into rosy mounds. His eyes were as blue as the mountain sky, and he had a prominent hunch to his back. "Can I help you?" he said, moving towards the cabin with a sack of logs under his arm.

"Uh . . ." I said, following his lead. "I'm looking for you. I think."

"Me?" he said, not slowing to stop. "And to what do I owe this honor?" The old man squatted and placed the sack of logs next to a pile of kindling to the side of the cabin and regarded me with curious eyes.

"Are you the old, wise man who lives up here?"

The old man stared right through me and arched a brow. "Do I look old to you?" he said.

"Oh . . . no . . . of course not," I said. My mouth was dry, and I was struggling to get the words out. "But I was told there was a wise man who lives on this mountain. A sage."

"Oh dear," he said, shaking his head in distaste. "I am afraid you have the wrong person."

"But you said you were the only person up here?"

He nodded. "I am," he said. "But I am no sage."

I regarded him with a blank expression.

"Nobody of such status would ever admit to being such a thing," he continued.

"Why not?" I asked.

"Because people expect too much from wise men," he continued, turning his head towards the heavens.

"Such as?"

"Answers," he said, looking back at me now. "Is that why you are here? For answers?" He narrowed his eyes and waited for my response.

"I guess so."

He nodded and then lifted a finger in the air. "Then you have proven my point."

The old man moved past me, towards another pile of logs stacked in one corner.

"There's more firewood over there . . ." he said. "If you wouldn't mind helping an *old* man."

He smiled a crooked smile, and I picked up some firewood and followed him into the cabin.

"You can put the logs down there," he continued, pointing towards a pile next to the hearth. "With the rest of them."

I squatted and placed the logs onto the pile.

"Can I offer you a drink?" he said.

"A water would be fine," I replied. "Thank you."

The old man reached for a pot on the side table, poured the liquid into a pewter mug, then passed it to me.

I winced as the liquid hit the back of my tongue.

"Cold, herbal tea," he said. "It's good for the soul."

"Thank you," I replied, wincing as I swallowed the concoction. It was disgusting.

"Better hot, though," he said, smiling again.

I set the empty mug down next to me. There was a fire going in the hearth, and the cabin had a rustic warmth to it. It was spartan in appearance and sparsely furnished: two threadbare chairs were angled before the fire; there was a table to the rear covered with an assortment of pots and pans; there were no pictures or tapestries on the walls; no signs of ornaments or curios on the shelves, and no clocks that I could hear.

"What time is it?" I asked.

"Time for a rest," the old man said, as he sat himself down

in the chair nearest the fire. "Why? Do you have somewhere to be?"

"No," I said, and I paused to gather my thoughts. "What is your name?"

"My name?" he said, "There's no need for names when you live alone up here." He yawned and stretched his legs out before the flames and gestured for me to take the seat next to him.

I stood for a moment and thought about leaving. The old man was strange, but what else was I expecting from someone who lived in isolation on a mountain. It was enough to test the sanest of minds. "But you *had* one..." I said, now taking a seat. "A name, that is?"

He nodded. "I had many names. But you can call me Virgil."

"I'm Hugo," I said. The chair creaked and strained as I leaned back into it.

"Have you come far?" Virgil said.

"Far enough, I guess."

"Well, I am sorry to disappoint you," he said. "But please stay for the night. It's nice to have some company once in a while." He kicked off his boots now and pointed his bare feet at the fire.

"Once in a while?" I said. "So you see other folk up here?"

Virgil chuckled to himself but said nothing.

"You *are* him. I know it! You are the old, wise man!"

With a tilt of the head, Virgil cast a sideways glance over his shoulder and pinned me to the wall with another stare. "Less of the *old*, please," he said. "Now, tell me why you have come here?"

I reached down for my rucksack beside me and took out the map inside my notebook. "I met a man," I said, leaning across to show him the map. "He came into the place I work and told me about you."

Virgil studied the map with one eye shut.

"He left this behind."

Virgil folded the map and passed it back to me. "It looks as though you're in the right place," he said. "According to this map, anyway."

"What do you mean?"

"What I mean is that you've come to the right place," he said. "But do you *really* know what you are seeking?"

I thought on it for a moment. "I'm not sure," I said.

"Think . . ." he said. "You have not traveled this far for no reason. Tell me what brings you here?" There was a long silence, and Virgil sat up in his chair and combed his beard with the ends of his fingers.

"It's complicated," I said.

"Is it?" he said. "Or are you trying to complicate something which, in reality, is quite simple?"

There was another silence between us, then I told the old man everything: about Donny's; about college and my future; about my parents, too. But I spoke nothing of Sarah; that was still too painful to think about.

"I don't know where I go from here," I said, "or who I want to be. I feel lost."

Virgil shook his head and said, "What you mean to say is that you don't know *who* you are?"

"No," I said. "I know who I am."

"Do you?" he said, as he leaned towards me. "Do you really?" His eyes flickered against the firelight and he studied me as though he was peering in to the deepest part of my soul.

"I'm Hugo . . ." I said.

"Yes, that is your name," he continued. "But is that all you are? A name among every other name out there?"

"I don't know," I said.

"You say you don't know what you want, yet you have

come here expecting someone else to answer the question for you . . . is that right?"

"I came here looking for guidance," I said, turning. "A meaning to all this."

"I see . . ." he said, running a finger through his beard again. "*Meaning*. It is a curious little word."

"How so?"

"It is the greatest question a person can ask, yet one which few ever understand."

I scratched my head and watched the fire burning in the hearth. "So, what is it? What is the meaning to all this?"

"To what?"

"All of it. *Life*."

The old man sighed and shook his head. "You're asking the wrong question."

"Then what is the right question?"

"It's not that one."

I rolled my eyes. "C'mon, enough with the riddles."

Virgil smiled, and for the first time, I saw a flash of teeth behind the thick, gray beard.

"How old are you?" he said.

"Nineteen."

"Nineteen . . ." he said. "There are many people much older than you that still ask this same question."

"Do you?"

It took the old man a moment to answer, but he never faltered in his response. "No," he said. "But you are young and expect answers to everything now without putting in the hard work." He rose from his chair and put another log on the fire.

"Then what should I do? Just sit and wait?"

"Oh no, that is the worst thing you could do," he replied, placing one hand on his hip as he straightened his back to stand again.

I sighed. "I feel like we're going round in circles here."

"I'll tell you what," he said, as he ambled towards the cabin door and reached for the handle. "I see you have a notebook with you. Why don't you write down the things you want from life in that? Perhaps then we can talk more."

He opened the cabin door, and I stood there for a moment, looking out onto sawtooth bluffs beneath a cobalt sky.

∼

JUST LIKE THE old man had asked, I found a spot in the sun on the edge of the cliff and put pen to paper. I sat for a long while and watched nothing but the shapes of clouds as they moved across the land below. And sometime later, when the jagged rocks cast long shadows in the half-light, I returned to the cabin with my notebook.

As I went to knock, the cabin door creaked open on its hinges, and Virgil stood with a grin on his face.

"Come in," he said. "I've made us some supper."

The old man had laid the table and there were two bowls at either end with what looked like chicken broth and rice. There was a mound of bread in the center, and two pewter mugs filled to the brim with the home brew he had given me earlier.

Virgil took a seat at one end, and I took the other, resting my notebook atop the table. The broth was the color of oatmeal, yet, despite its appearance, it tasted divine.

As I took up my spoon, I looked down at the liquid in my mug placed next to it.

"Don't worry," Virgil said. "The tea is hot this time."

We ate in silence, and as I gulped down the last of the broth, Virgil glanced up at me.

"Did you finish making notes?" he said.

I nodded, then placed my spoon back down into my empty bowl.

"What did you write?"

I slid my notebook across the table, and Virgil opened it to the first page. He looked at it for no longer than a few seconds, tore out the page I had written, closed the cover, then placed it back down on the table in front. He kept the torn page for himself and slipped it into his pocket.

"Why did you do that?" I said.

"Why did you write these?" he replied.

I regarded him with bewilderment. "Because you told me to," I said.

"But why did you write these things in particular?" he asked, wiping his mouth with a napkin. "Wealth. Recognition. Reputation. Happiness. Why these?"

"Isn't that want everyone wants?"

"Never mind anyone else. Why do *you* want these?"

"I want to have a good life."

"I see," he said, folding his hands together in his lap. "Go on . . ."

"Money gives you choices," I continued. "Recognition brings success. Reputation gives me influence—"

"And what about happiness?" he said.

"If I live a good life, I must be happy," I said. "Fulfilled."

"I agree with you," he said.

"You do?"

"Yes," he replied. "But do you really believe that someone who does not have those things on your list is not happy in their life?"

A silence hung in the air as I pondered on it. "I don't know," I said. "Perhaps they're not as happy as someone who *does* have them."

Virgil brushed the bread crumbs from his chest and

looked about the walls and ceiling of the cabin. "Look around you," he said. "Do I have these things?"

The old man was not a wealthy man, that much was obvious. And he lived alone, without another soul to so much as look at, let alone talk to. I wasn't sure how anyone could be happy like this.

"I guess not," I said, leaning back in my chair now.

"Then if you want all these things, why have you come here? Do I look like someone who knows anything about these things you desire?"

"No, I guess not."

The fire cracked in the hearth as Virgil finished his meal. "Answer me this," he said. "If you had to choose out of all those things on your list, which would it be?"

"Why do I have to choose?"

"Because life is about making choices."

"So it's not possible to have them all?"

"Maybe it is," he said, shaking his head as he stood with his bowl in his hands. "Maybe you will have all those things someday. But maybe not. It's a hypothetical question, but humor an old man will you. Choose one." He got to his feet and carried our empty bowls over to the wash area.

"Happiness," I said. "All the other things mean nothing without happiness. I'd choose that."

"Good," he said, as he ushered me over to a shelf in the corner stacked high with tattered blankets and patchwork eiderdowns. He removed a thick coverlet from the pile, handed it to me, then showed me to the door.

"Where are we going?" I said.

"Nowhere," he said, as he stood by the door. "You can sleep in the barn for the night. I am afraid I have no room for guests in here."

"That's it?" I said, scrunching my face up into a ball.

The old man looked at me with a deadpan expression. "Were you expecting more?" he said.

"I haven't come all this way to sleep in a barn!"

"I am afraid you have. But I think you'll find the barn more pleasant than sleeping outside. The nights get cold up here."

I stood there and glared at him and heaved a sigh. "You really aren't the wise man, are you?"

"I never pretended to be," he replied, and his face showed no sign of anything.

We looked at one another for a moment, but I could see that there was something in his eye. Something hidden behind the flashes of blue. Something willing.

"There's something you're not telling me . . ." I said.

"Goodnight," he said, as he opened the door.

I stepped out into the cold mountain breeze with the coverlet under my arm and nothing but the moon to light the way. I turned back to face the old man once more. "What do I have to do for you to help me?"

Virgil placed a hand on my right shoulder and let it linger for a moment. "Help yourself," he said. "However, I will offer you this only once, because I can see something in you. But only if this is what you really want?"

"Yes," I said. "I do."

The old man plucked two silver keys from his pocket and dropped them into my hand.

"Stay with me," he said. "Just for a few days. And maybe you will find the answers you are seeking."

One key was just like any regular key, but the other had a long stem and a red jewel encrusted into the bow. It was old. Very old.

"One of those keys opens the door to the barn," Virgil continued. "Make yourself at home."

"And the other one?"

With a gentle push on my back, Virgil gestured towards the barn. "You will have to find out another time," he said. "We'll start tomorrow."

And with that, he retreated into his cabin and closed the door on the world.

CHAPTER 5

I woke the next morning with a stiff neck and scruffs of hair at all angles and surrounded by drying logs and various tools and oddments which hung from hooks on the timber walls. I had slept on a straw mattress in the hayloft, and the barn was cold and had the earthy scent of sawn lumber.

The night had been long, and my eyes were sore and leaden. I had been awake for much of it, unable to find a comfortable position to rest my head, then listening to the faraway caterwauls of coyotes or wolves as they carried across the mountain. And in the moments before I had drifted into sleep, the wind had started up and continued through the night, and the token rest I had managed was shallow and broken.

Virgil was bent double in front of me as I opened the barn door, sprinkling feed on the ground where a dozen chickens were roaming, free from their coop. The morning wind had a bite to it, and my hands were frozen to the bone.

"Good morning," Virgil said, still scattering the feed at his feet. He wore the face of a man who rose with the sun, fresh and spry, unlike my own. "A late riser, I see."

I rubbed my eyes and yawned beneath a ginger sky. Daybreak was barely upon us, but I had already lost all sense of time.

Virgil came over with a cup of steaming tea, which I sipped with caution. The herbal concoction had a bitter taste to it, even when hot, and I grimaced as I swallowed.

"That'll wake you up," he said, as he lifted his own empty cup.

I sipped on the tea and let out a sigh, and I could see my breath in the mountain air.

Virgil stood like an ancient monument with his hands behind his back. "Drink up," he continued.

He watched me until I drank my cup dry, and I remarked the fullness in his cheeks. The old man stood with sturdier bearing, stout on his feet, and there was less of a hunch in his back.

When he finished with the chickens, we retired to the cabin and ate eggs and fried bread for breakfast.

"What are we doing today?" I said.

"The coops need cleaning out," he said, soaking up the egg yolk on his plate with the last morsel of bread.

I said nothing, but feigned a smile.

"Is that a problem for you?" he continued.

"No," I said, but the displeasure on my face betrayed my words. I was never any good at hiding my feelings; it was a trait I had inherited from my mother.

"Good," he replied, "then you might as well make a start on it if you're finished here . . ."

∽

FIVE MINUTES later and I was mucking out the chicken

coops, replacing the sodden straw with clean bedding from the barn, and sweeping up any mess I could find. I worked hard and fast, and once I'd finished, I made my way back to the cabin and knocked on the door.

"No need to knock," came the voice from the other side. "Come in."

As I entered, I saw Virgil sat at ease in his chair reading a book by the fire. *My book*.

"This is a fascinating read," he said. He put the copy of *Robinson Crusoe* down on his lap and lifted his head to look at me.

"Now what?" I asked, my hands brown with muck.

"Now you can clean this place," he replied, looking about the cabin. "I haven't done it for some time."

My jaw fell open. "You're not serious, right?"

"Do I look like I'm joking?"

He didn't. His face was flat, yet somehow earnest.

"But I'm ready to learn," I said. "Whatever it is you need to teach me . . ."

"And this is your first lesson," he said.

"How so?"

Virgil got to his feet now. "Because the first step on this journey of yours is to learn to take ownership of your actions," he said. "We all have chores to do. It is not bad for you. You merely believe this is a lousy request because you feel entitled to something better. Like you deserve something greater. But we all have our chores."

"But I already cleaned the coops."

He shrugged his shoulders and came towards me. "Yet there is always more to do," he continued. "I have offered you a place to stay, and, as much as I am sure I will enjoy your company, there is still work to be done. And considering how you were kind enough to remind me how old I am getting, I couldn't think of a better person to do the job instead."

"But there *is* no one else."

"Then it looks as though you came at the right time." The old man smiled now. "I will be back in an hour," he said, heading for the door.

"Where are you going?"

"I was watching you earlier . . ." he said. "You left the chickens out, so I will finish what you started." He arched a brow and pursed his lips. "Perhaps you will do a better job on this task."

Virgil left, and the door closed hard behind him.

I stood there, broom in hand, determined to prove the old man wrong. His words had carried a sting so strong, and I got busy dusting the tables, cleaning the drawers, wiping the shelves, and sweeping the dirt from the floor. And, for just a moment, it seemed like I was back at Donny's again.

∼

As I finished stacking the plates in the cupboard, Virgil came back into the cabin and perused the place, taking a moment to inspect my hard work. "Better," he said.

The last plate near damn fell from my hand as I glared at him. "Better?" I said. "The place is spotless!"

"It is," he replied, running a finger along the top shelf nearest to him. There was not a speck of dust to behold. "I'm sorry, were you expecting some kind of reward for your efforts?"

"A little gratitude wouldn't go amiss."

"Chores are a thankless task," he said. "And what greater reward is there than the sense of ownership and accomplishment that comes from doing a good deed."

"If you say so," I said.

Virgil grinned. "Come with me."

I followed him outside and watched him take up the rifle leaning against the side of the cabin.

"The first step to living a happy and meaningful life, is to take ownership of the things you can control," he said, leading me towards a small trail hidden at the far end of the plateau on which the cabin stood. "Even a simple task, like cleaning, is rewarding when you take ownership and pride in what you do."

When I thought about it, I figured the old man was right. You could view any mundane task as a chore, but if you took pride in it, as if it were your duty, there was something satisfying about a job well done.

We clambered down a steep slope lined with fresh paw marks in the earth. Whatever lived up here with the old man seemed to travel on four legs. Virgil caught me bending down to study them.

"We get coyotes up here from time to time," he said. "It's nothing to worry about."

I nodded and got to my feet again. "Where are we going?"

"You will see."

As we reached the foot of the mountain, Virgil lifted the brim on his oilskin bucket hat and pointed a finger to the west. "It's this way," he said.

He led me to a small clearing beyond a copse of yellow-leafed cottonwoods and found a discreet spot by a pile of rocks where he laid down the rifle. He squatted in the dirt and put a finger to his lips to declare a silence and told me to watch and only watch. But there was nothing but grassland all around us and the twitter of songbirds in the trees.

I sat there, listening to the birdsong and picking the dirt from my fingernails, and, some time later, Virgil nudged my arm and pointed at something in the distance.

As I followed his gaze, I could see a flash of brown fur

moving through the thicket in the distance, then a white-tailed deer and her fawn emerged from the tree line and wandered out through the clearing where they grazed on the bottle-green grass.

"We're short on food," Virgil said, placing the stock of the rifle in my hands. He pressed a hand to my back and used the top of a boulder to steady the barrel and leaned into my ear with a whisper. "Have you ever shot a gun before?"

"Yes," I said, pressing the butt of the rifle into the nook of my shoulder. "My dad used to take me hunting when I was a child. But that was a long time ago, and I never liked it much."

"Okay," he said, keeping his voice low, and he pushed my head down so my eye was level with the scope. "You have a choice to make: either you go hungry for the next few days, or you can take the shot. But you only have the one."

My forehead beaded with sweat. "Which one should we take?" I said.

"That's for you to decide. The mother, or the baby."

I put my right eye to the scope and steadied my breathing. The doe looked up, startled by the crack of a falling branch somewhere in the forest. She was stock-still, alert, her eyes scanning the trees for peril. And when satisfied there was none, she lowered her head and continued feeding on the grass.

Virgil hunkered down beside me. "If you take the mother, then the baby will be too young to survive on its own. But if you take the baby, then you will have taken a life in its infancy, and the mother may be too old to birth any more young."

I swallowed dry and leveled the barrel of the rifle from mother to baby and then back again.

"Make your choice," Virgil said.

"I can't . . ." I said, the sweat rolling down my cheek now. "I don't want to take the shot."

"You *must* choose one," Virgil said.

I wiped the sweat on the collar of my shirt, then put my eye against the scope again. I leveled the crosshairs on the fawn's body, right below the heart, pushed forward on the safety lever, and let my finger fall onto the trigger.

∾

GUNFIRE RIPPED THROUGH THE STILLNESS, and the fawn bucked and twisted, then disappeared behind the tall grass as it fell to its death. The doe bolted for the safety of the tree line and disappeared as quick as she had surfaced.

Virgil stood and cleared his throat, then went over to collect the fallen fawn.

I stayed back, unable to watch, imbued with a sense of sadness.

Virgil returned, carrying the fawn over his shoulders. "Gather your things," he said.

∾

"I CAN SEE that was hard for you," Virgil said, as we started back up the trail towards the cabin.

"Yes," I said. "You made me feel as though I had no choice."

"You always have a choice," he said. "You made a decision —to eat—and now you must learn to live with the consequences of that decision."

I scratched my chin as I turned back to look at the deserted clearing behind me. "But *you* made me do it . . ."

"You should not be so easily influenced by others," he said. "After all, I did not pull the trigger."

"I don't understand what this is about?"

"It is about taking ownership of your decisions, and learning to accept them, whatever the outcome," Virgil replied. "Not just this one, but the decisions you make each day, perhaps unknowingly."

"Such as?"

"Such as the ones from your past," he continued. "Such as not getting into college, or losing your job. Such as this girl kissing another man."

I stopped dead in my tracks. "How do you know about Sarah? I never told you about her."

The old man lifted his head to see my face. "It was in your notebook," he said.

"You read my notebook?" My body was quaking now.

"I thought it would be sensible to get to know one another. And what better way than to read your innermost thoughts."

"You don't have any right to go through my notebook!"

Virgil sighed. "Listen to me. You came here to solicit my advice," he said. "So here it is: you didn't ask to lose your job, or your girlfriend. But she is not deserving of your love. And your job, well, is just a job."

"That's easy for you to say."

"And it will be for you, when you learn to own the choices you make in life."

We continued up the trail until the old man stopped for breath. He inhaled sharply, then pressed on. I followed closely behind.

"I don't understand what it is you're trying to tell me," I said.

Virgil slowed and came beside me. "You are not in control of other people's actions," he said. "Not this girl, or your boss, or anyone else for that matter. And no amount of worrying or regret will change that. Life will throw many challenges your way, most of which you cannot change. But the one thing you *can* control is how you respond and rise to these challenges. Taking ownership of your decisions is the first step. To do so is honorable, and honor brings respect. For yourself. And from others."

As we neared the top of the trail, Virgil stopped once again, this time to perch on some rocks which overlooked the blanket of green land below. "You must remember that life is not indebted to you; it owes you nothing. No more than it does the next man," he said, pulling two red apples out from the satchel he was carrying.

He handed one to me, and I took a seat next to him.

"You must learn to remove your self-entitlements," he continued, biting into the side of his apple. "Life does not owe you to be wealthy, healthy, happy, or successful. We do not deserve special treatment. Nature views everyone with indifference.

"So, you must take responsibility for these hardships that have befallen you, be it your actions, or your judgments, because your pain and your sorrow is a reminder of your duty to own each decision you have made along the way, whatever the outcome.

"If you are unhappy, it is because of you. If you are resentful, it is you. If you are without purpose, it is you, and only ever *you*. Own your decisions first, and only then should you look to question."

"And how do I do that?"

"Be honest with yourself and accept that you are not without your faults. More often than not you will have seen your misfortunes coming, but you ignored the signs. Other people will often let you know of their feelings in the subtlest of ways."

The old man was right, I'd seen Donny's letters on his desk weeks ago, and I'd noticed Sarah had been distancing herself from me since she'd started speaking about a new friend of hers. These were all signs, and I'd ignored every one.

Virgil finished eating his apple and said, "Stop pretending to *be* someone else *for* someone else. It will never get you far." He stopped for breath and patted me hard on the back. "This girl wanted someone else, not you. That's fine for her, but you have no control over that. She is the one who will have to live with her own decisions, just like you do."

We continued up the last part of the trail towards the log cabin, and Virgil was slow yet steady on his feet as he shouldered the carcass.

"Your parents wish for you to tread a certain path they have marked out for you, that much is clear. But for what?" he said, as we walked side by side. "So they can be proud that the man they created eluded the failures in their own lives? So they can convince themselves that the decisions and choices they made as parents were the right ones all along?

"You want to make them proud, of course you do, but do not be a pretender. Be genuine. Do not live in this ego-driven world and play a show for others. You will never be enough for this one girl. You may never live to be the man your parents imagined. But own those facts and stop pretending. Show them something else they can be proud of by being genuine. And if you do that, you will be enough for someone else one day."

As we made our way up to the cabin, Virgil set down the carcass and went over to the henhouse, and, as I watched him tend to his chickens, I realized that all of this had been a test.

I had killed that deer. But, as sad as I felt, it did not matter whether I had pulled the trigger. The lesson he had tried to teach me was that I had to own my decision either way, even if it was one I did not wish to make.

The first lesson was to own my decisions; my actions, and my judgments, as they were the only things I could control.

As Virgil made his way towards the cabin, he turned back to face me. "I need to do some work inside," he said. "Let's meet back here later. Take some time to think about what I said."

I nodded and smiled, and the old man smiled back as he stepped inside.

"And thank you," he said. "The place is spotless."

CHAPTER 6

The sun was down when I heard a knock on the barn door and I opened it to see Virgil stood with an oil lamp hanging from one hand.

"I've made a stew, if you would like to join me?" he said, his face aglow in the lamplight.

We sat at the table in the cabin, and Virgil took a slice of bread from the basket, then passed it to me. And we filled our bellies with the hot stew he had made.

"Have you thought about what I said earlier?" Virgil said.

"Yes," I replied. "The first lesson is about taking ownership of my decisions and actions and accepting the things that have already happened."

"And have you?"

"There were signs . . ." I said, nodding in approval. "And I ignored them. I realize now that I feel trapped because I'm trying to be someone I am not. Like you said before, life owes me nothing. Nothing which I do not already owe to myself, anyway."

"Good," he said, "then I think you are ready for the next step."

After we finished our supper, Virgil led me outside to look at the stars, and we stepped out into the cold night of the mountain and sat under a coal-black, stellar sky. And for a while we did nothing but watch the shimmer of far-flung orbs and the glow of the midnight moon as we perched on the rocks on the high bluff overlooking nothing but darkness below.

"It is only when you take ownership of your decisions and actions, and accept things as they come, that you can seek to question what gives you fulfillment and purpose in life," he said, lifting a cup of warm tea to his lips. "Listen carefully, because this is one of the toughest lessons one must learn . . ."

Virgil reached into his pocket and withdrew the slip of paper that he had torn from my notebook the night before. I sat up to face him and listened.

"This is the list you wrote last night . . ." he said, as he tore the paper into a dozen more pieces and cast it out into the mountain wind. "You have come here to learn the secrets of meaning and happiness, is that right?"

"Yes," I replied.

"And if I sent you on your way now, would you feel any different about it? Would you feel happier?"

"Probably not."

"Which tells you one thing," he said. "That coming here has not made you happier. It has not made you wealthy, successful, or celebrated . . . is this true?"

"I guess so."

"That's because the happiness you seek is to be found only in a fool's paradise," he continued. "It is a life where you satisfy your ego in pursuit of material and senseless things. It is a life of indulgence and greed. It is a life ruled by fears and desires. It is a life in pursuit of pleasure and avoiding pain. It is all of these things."

"How so?"

"Look at it this way," he said. "We feel pain when we fall victim to our fears, or cannot achieve what our heart's desire. And we feel pleasure from avoiding what we fear most, and in fulfilling those same desires. But we must keep these sentiments in check, as they contribute to the illusion of happiness as you understand it. Because true happiness comes from someplace else."

"Where?"

"First," he said, lifting his head to observe the inky welkin above us. "I will tell you where it does not come from. You will not find happiness in any foreign land. You will not find it at the bottom of the deepest ocean. You will not find it at the peak of the highest mountain, nor at the edge of any barren desert. You will not even find it at the farthest reaches on a distant sun."

The stars were huge and plentiful and we sat and watched them as they scintillated like cloistered beacons in the darkness.

"So, tell me again, are you any happier now you have found me here on this mountain?" Virgil asked.

I shook my head and said, "No."

"That is because happiness is not a journey's end, but the journey itself," he said. "For this reason you should not make happiness your goal. Better to pursue something else . . ."

"My purpose?"

"Yes."

"And that's why I'm here," I said. "Because I do not know where to find it . . ."

We stepped down from the bluff, and Virgil got a fire going outside with some dry wood from the barn.

"You are restless because you search for meaning and fulfillment in places where they cannot be found," he said, as he stoked the fire to get it burning. "And many people do the same which is why they move from one thing to another, forever chasing something which they will never find. And these people will never find it because they never knew what they were searching for in the first place.

"So, to ask what the meaning of life is, is to ask the wrong question. For the answer is in the question itself."

"What is it?"

"The meaning of life is to live a *meaningful* life: one pursuing your purpose; one where you live the best version of yourself on each new day; one where you fulfill your potential as a human being in each of the roles you undertake in life. As a son, or partner, or father, or friend. Because if you woke up tomorrow as the only person left on this world, you would realize that there must also be something greater than just your own existence. It is the existence of all else, and how it works together, that brings meaning to our lives."

I moved towards the fire and let the notion sink in for a moment. "But what if there is a higher purpose to all this?" I said.

"There might be," Virgil said. "I am not God. But if you view anything outside your own actions or judgments as the source of true meaning, then you will forever live a life of restlessness and searching."

Virgil started pacing about the fire now as I watched.

"The meaning of life has become lost," he continued. "Many assume that their purpose is to pursue nothing other than a more comfortable standard of living. Chasing wealth and reputation and fame has become life's goal for these people. These are the things they believe give them a reason to live, but these same people have forgotten what they're truly living for, because the only good is that which comes from ourselves. Everything else is indifferent."

I warmed my hands against the heat of the flames and

said, "What do you mean when you say that everything else is indifferent?"

"Let me tell you a story," he said. "Three women went out for a cup of tea one day at a fancy parlor in the city. When the waiter came out, he produced three types of cups from which the women could drink their tea from. One cup was made from paper, the other was china, and the last cup was made from rare crystal. Each of the women, beguiled by its beauty, chose the crystal cup.

"A man sat next to the women then asked them why they chose the crystal cups, and all three women agreed that the crystal was more graceful and luxurious than the paper and china cups. The man then smiled and finished his own tea, which he had drank from the paper cup. The three women laughed and asked the man why he would drink from the paper cup when he could have chosen the crystal like them. The man then stood to leave and said, 'The crystal is exquisite, I agree, but all I ever wanted was the tea.'"

I nodded and raised a smile as I sipped my own cup of warm tea with renewed appreciation.

"It is often our nature to place greater value in the things we believe will make us happy, that we often forget what we wanted in the first place," Virgil continued. "Unhappiness flows from places where we care more about the things we do not control; the things that we assume will bring us happiness, and in the images of a perfect life that we carve out in our mind's eye.

"You will not find happiness in trappings and worldly goods, nor in prestige or wealth. The difference between the wise man and the fool is that the wise man needs and wants for nothing, but makes use of things that he already has. The fool, on the other hand, needs and wants for more and more, yet makes no good with any of it.

"A man may pursue wealth, but is he rich if he is not

happy with his lot? We are so consumed by pursuing the things we do not have out there, in the world, that we lose sight of the things that we can achieve from ourselves. Our judgments create desires, and our desires create ambitions to pursue the things that we seldom need.

"Of course, if you had a choice, you would rather be rich than poor, or respected than reviled, or healthy than sick. That is normal. But these are nothing more than preferred states of living, and happiness is not lost on those bereft of these fortunes."

"Our health, wealth, and reputation can be used for both good and evil," he continued. "Virtue and vice. If used virtuously, they can add to one's physical comfort in life. But if used for vice, then they will only lead you to a place of wretchedness, for these things, and man's possessions, are nothing more than life's trappings. You must learn to unburden yourself from life's burdens, and all these external things, because, as I have said, happiness is not a destination or a state of mind: it is living from moment to moment, enduring the adventure in pursuit of your purpose.

"It is the reason the wealthy man pursues more wealth: he enjoys the chase. This tells you that wealth alone does not make him happy. It is also why the powerful pursue more power. But instead of wealth and power, the wisest of men pursue something else: they pursue wisdom and purpose."

I held my arms against my chest as my body shuddered from the cold. "Then I should pursue nothing other than my own purpose?" I said.

Virgil nodded and ran a hand across his silver beard. "If today was your last day on this earth, would you go looking for a bigger house, or a new car? Would you care for riches and wealth?" he said. "No, because in your heart you know these things can only aid in your physical comfort in the journey of life. They are not the things you really value most.

You came into this world with nothing, and you will leave with nothing, because you were born with all the tools that you ever needed to live a happy life.

"If you pursue the road of purpose, then happiness will join you for the ride, because happiness is nothing more than the fruits of living a meaningful and fulfilled life—"

"From being the best person I can be?" I said. "From focusing only on what *I* can control?"

"Correct," Virgil replied, as he lifted a hand to the heavens and plucked a star from the sable sky between two fingers as if it were a magician's trick. "You will never feel fulfilled without a purpose in life. And you will never know your purpose without knowing yourself."

As he lowered his hand again, I could see the shimmer of a silver coin tumble in his palm.

"Only *you* can be the person you want to be," he said, handing me the coin. "Don't let anyone else tell you otherwise."

As he dropped the silver coin into my hand, I could tell that it looked like no other coin I had seen before. It was round, like any other coin, but it was smooth and featureless on both sides, and felt like the weight of a ten coins combined. And its surface shimmered as bright as the stars themselves.

"Carry this coin as a reminder," Virgil said. "A reminder that what you seek is not out there, amongst the stars, but was right here, in your hands, all along."

As Virgil returned to the cabin, I stood alone in the blackness for a long while, looking down at the coin. And then I returned to the straw mattress for a bed, and laid still on my back, listening to the sounds of the wind again. I could not sleep. I felt alive for the first time I could remember. And I told myself that, when I woke tomorrow, I would not ask what life can do for me; rather what *I* can do for life.

CHAPTER 7

The next morning I had packed my rucksack and left it beside the entrance to the barn as I went to meet Virgil at the edge of the high bluff, watching the sun breach the curve of the horizon.

"You are earlier today," he said, as I approached.

"Do you ever sleep?" I replied.

Virgil chortled and turned to face me. "I like to come here before daybreak and reflect on the day ahead," he said. "That way I can prepare for anything that might come my way."

The sky was a crimson red, and we stood and watched the veil of blackness lift from the mountainside.

"Are you leaving?" he asked.

"Yes," I said. "I feel you have taught me what I needed to know."

"Is that so?" he replied, arching a brow. "But we have only just begun. There is much left to learn."

As I studied his face, I noticed that he looked younger still this morning. The creases on his face had withered to faint lines, and his hair looked thicker, with shoots of russet and gold amongst the gray.

"By all means," he continued, turning back to face the vista below, "leave if you must. But you are far from ready."

I kicked the rocks under my feet and sighed. "What is next then?" I asked.

"You have learned the value of taking ownership of your actions and decisions in your life, and that you must accept the past for what it is. You are aware of the universal misunderstanding as to the things that bring genuine joy and happiness to people's lives," he said. "But the next step is to understand *why* we make the decisions we do, and *how* to take the right action, equipped with this knowledge."

As Virgil took a step back from the edge of the bluff, he removed his oilskin bucket hat from his pocket and pulled it over his head. And, for the first time, I saw something familiar about him. It was a sideways smile that I had seen before. It was just like my grandfather's smile; now nothing more than a treasured memory. And his eyes were also like my grandfather's too, as deep and as blue as the ocean depths.

Virgil stepped away from the cliff edge and reached for a wooden stick propped up against the side of the cabin. "Lets go," he said, using the stick to steady himself.

"Where are we going?"

"I must deliver a parcel to an old acquaintance in the next town."

"In Meridian?"

"No, it is on a different road," he replied, "and the journey will be long."

"How far is it?"

"It will take most of the day, but perhaps you would care to join me?" He waited for my response.

"Okay," I said, "I'll come with you."

Virgil returned to the cabin and came back a minute later

dragging an old knapsack over the rough ground. "Put this on," he said.

I heaved a sigh and put on the knapsack laden with oddments, and Virgil led me down the trail towards the foot of the mountain.

∼

WE DESCENDED TO THE BOTTOM, down past the jagged cliffs and steep slopes, and happened upon a large meadow brimming with pink and purple fireweed. From there, we followed the trail west, along a broken track and over alpine grasslands, until we reached a fork in the path which gave way to two bridges on either side of a clear creek.

I stopped for breath, panting hard. My shirt was sodden, but Virgil had barely broken a sweat.

"Take that off your back and let us drink," he said.

I removed the knapsack and let it fall to the ground and sat and drank from the flask when Virgil had taken his share. For a while we basked in the heat of the noontime sun and ate some dry cornbread for sustenance.

"Which way do we go?" I said, realizing that there were no signposts at the fork in the path

"What do you think?" Virgil replied.

I regarded him with a puzzled look. "You have no idea where we are, do you?"

He shrugged his shoulders as I devoured the last crumb of cornbread.

"It's been a long time since I traveled this way," he said.

"Are you kidding?"

"No," he replied. "Why don't you decide."

I looked daggers at him. "How am I supposed to know when I don't even know where we're going?"

We sat there for a moment longer, and Virgil smiled to himself.

"Why are you smiling?" I said.

"I remember now," he said. "Both paths lead to the same place. It just depends which one you would prefer to take."

"What is the quickest way?"

"This way," he said, as he pointed to the path on the left.

"Then let's go that way."

"But the other path is less steep, if I remember rightly."

I got to my feet and stood before the old man. "Is this one of your tests?" I said.

He grinned again and stood to join me. "As I told you before, we must all make decisions in life. And, fate permitting, we make the best ones. But fate does not always smile upon us.

"You will have to make some hard decisions in your life to come. Some you will decide on the spur of the moment, and others with great contemplation. Some decisions you make will be the right one, and others not so."

He moved passed me and stood where the trail diverged.

"Some decisions will be dear to your heart," he continued. "Like which bridges to cross, and which ones to burn. When to conform, and when to object. When to take less, and when to offer more. When to fight greed to gain something greater. When to tackle the past, and when to forget it. When to let go, or when to try harder. When to say yes, and when to say no."

I joined him and looked down both paths to the left and right of me. "Okay," I said. "So how do I know which is the right path?"

"You don't. That is the beauty of it," he replied. "Why would you want to? All you can do is think on it and go with what your heart tells you."

He looked at me and pointed to the path to the left. "You

wanted to take this route because it appears easier?" he said. "Because you are struggling with the load on your back?" He glanced down at the knapsack laid out on the ground before us.

"I guess so."

"But every day you carry a different load and taking the shortcut means you might miss other opportunities you had not considered. You do not grow stronger carrying this weight if you always take the easy road." Virgil turned and pointed towards the trail on the left again. "Imagine that this path leads you to all the wealth and fame you ever desired. You would be the envy of all men, and society would revere you. And, with this foresight, you would know every move you need to make along the way, and every decision you had to reach to get there. But, what you will never know, is whether all this fame and wealth will make you happy at the end. Would you still want to cross this same bridge?"

"I'm not sure," I said. "It would have to be worth it in the end."

"Every bridge you cross, and every path after it, comes with its own uncertainties. But, when *you* want what *someone else* wants, or what *others* tell you is good, you become enslaved to that very person or thing they desire." Virgil turned and pointed to the path to the right now. "However, you have a second option," he continued. "You could take this other path. You will still never know what awaits you at the end, or along the way, but you can learn to enjoy the journey for the mystery that it is.

"The road may be hard. There will be many obstacles in your path. But you will feel a sense of fulfillment because you had the strength to face those obstacles, and, with each conquest, the load on your back grows lighter. Now, tell me, which path do you wish to take?"

I pondered on it for a long while and then pointed to the path to the right.

"The truth is," he said, smiling to himself again. "There is only ever one path."

"How come?"

Virgil lifted the rim of his hat and squinted against the sun. "Do you play chess?" he asked.

"Sometimes."

"Well, life is much like chess. We enjoy the challenge of the game, even though there is a risk we may lose. But the reason we delight in it is that we understand the limitations and rules of the game. We make moves, and those moves have consequences. We try to think several steps ahead and convince ourselves that we are in control of the game. But we can only ever think so far ahead.

"We try to plot our successes by moving pieces into play. Sometimes we win; other times we're checkmated. Life is no different, and when we can accept the rules and limitations of life, we can learn to enjoy the game."

Virgil looked down at me and pulled me by my shoulders to face him. "I cannot plot your path for you, I can only point you to the one worth taking."

"But if everything is fated, and always supposed to be a certain way, then does it really matter?" I said.

Virgil pursed his lips. "Fate does not happen regardless of your actions. It happens *because* of them."

As I looked down the two paths on either side, I felt a renewed energy surge through my legs. "Then let's go on," I said.

∾

WE TOOK the path on the right and the journey was long and hard and what seemed like no end. As the afternoon sun fell in the west, we crossed through a dense thicket of towering maples and cottonwoods, and over field upon field of rough ground.

"We must keep going," Virgil said, as I struggled behind. "We need to make it before sundown."

We picked up another trail as we reached a small grove of pine trees beyond some hills, and we marched until we reached a dusty highway where I could finally see the tops of roofs in the distance.

A ragged mesa flanked the road on one side, and the rock face was etched with time-worn scars.

"They say a tribe used to live in these hills many years ago," Virgil said, as walked shoulder to shoulder. "And legend has it, if you listen closely, you can sometimes hear the echoes of their voices on a quiet night."

"And you believe in that?" I said.

"I believe anything is possible, just like I believe the actions of one man can live on forevermore, as though it were a voice itself, carried across oceans from wind to wind."

I glanced over the looming hills and imagined a dozen eyes looking down at us from unseen places above, their faces chalked behind the scrub as they carried their primitive weapons of war. "Can I ask you a question?" I said.

"Go on," Virgil replied.

"Do you have any regrets?"

But the old man did not answer. He just grinned and lifted a hand to shield his eyes from the sun. "We are almost there."

The town was deep in the tall timbers, and although the view of distant buildings came as a welcome sight, it felt far removed from what I had come to know.

I limped with each step now, and as I peered up, I could see the black and white wings of a hawk circling above our heads as we neared our destination.

"She has traveled a long way, like us," Virgil said, looking skyward at the gliding raptor.

"How do you know?"

"You learn to understand that nature has its ways. This bird will fly many miles looking for food," he continued. "But she is smart enough to use nature to her advantage, without ever taking from it."

"How do you mean?"

"You see how she does not flap her wings? That is because she uses columns of warm air from the ground to keep her soaring as she searches for prey below. This way she can travel great distances without using much energy. She is in perfect harmony with nature."

"That *is* smart," I said.

"She is, but she is no smarter than you. She simply knows how to make better use of her surroundings," he continued. "We all possess an instinctive knowledge, but knowledge alone, without action, is like that hawk without its wings."

I reached a hand back to grab the flask of water from the knapsack's side pocket. There was just enough water for a single mouthful.

"Finish it," Virgil said. "You need it more than I do."

I swilled down the last of the water, then returned the empty flask to its pocket.

"The hawk must fly to live," Virgil continued. "She cannot sit still and wait for food to come to her, or she will die. The hawk knows she can fly, but if she chooses not to, whether out of fear, judgment, or laziness, then she has failed as a hawk, and as nature has intended for her. To that end, she must act; not just to survive, but to thrive. Without question, she knows her purpose, for it always existed in her heart."

My feet were sore and blistered by the time we reached the dusty streets of Albion, a small town nestled in the foothills of a forgotten land. To the east lay forests of pines and aspens, and to the north and west the town was bordered by grassy knolls.

The sun was high as we came in, and the main thoroughfare was lined with tumbledown shops and small concerns. Despite that, a hundred people filled the walkways, going about their daily business.

As we came to rest outside a grocery store, Virgil stepped behind me and removed something from the knapsack.

"I'll be back shortly," he said.

"Where are you going?"

"To do what I came here to do."

I could see now that he was holding a parcel bound with string.

"Take a look around," he said. "I'll meet you back here in an hour."

I watched Virgil turn down a narrow alley, and I crossed the road to the other side and found a spot in the shade under a giant cedar to rest my feet. I placed the knapsack down beside me and took out my notebook and pen and began to write with the pitter-patter of footsteps and the chugging of engines around me.

∽

When I looked up again, I saw a girl with auburn hair step out from the grocery store across the road, carrying two bags in either hand. She was young, of even age to me, and wore a blue dress with white polka-dots which hung about her knees. She was beautiful.

She struggled with the grocery bags as she made her way

up the hill towards a tree-lined street, and I heaved the knapsack onto my back once more and followed her at a clip.

"Can I help you with that?" I said, now within earshot.

She turned, and her eyes went wide as she saw me coming up behind, then smiled a smile as warm as the evening sun which took shape over the arid hills to the west. Her red hair glistened in the half-light.

"Oh, thanks . . ." she said. "I've not seen you before. Are you new around here?"

"I'm passing through," I said.

We stood toe to toe for a moment, then I reached down to take a bag from either hand. As she leaned towards me, I could smell the sweetness of strawberries on a summer's day.

"Where are you headed?" I said.

"Not far," she replied. "Just a few more streets up this hill."

∽

SHE TOLD me her name was Sophia as we walked together, and I told her mine, which raised another smile.

"Sorry," she said, stifling a laugh, "but my dog's called Hugo, too."

"Really?" I said. "Well, it's a fitting name for a dog, I suppose."

"Yes, it is," she replied, and she chuckled now. "I chose it."

Her eyes fell to the floor, and there was a lump in my throat. My mouth was as dry as the dirt path, and I struggled to find my next words.

"In fact, you don't look too dissimilar . . ." she continued, ending the uncomfortable silence.

I looked at her and pulled a face. "Hang on . . ." I said. "Are you comparing me to your dog?"

"I think it's the hair," she continued. "It's kind of straggly like his."

My cheeks burned as I tried to flick the hair out of my face. "Sorry," I said.

"Don't be, I like it," she said.

Her skin was a pale brown, and I counted six freckles on her left cheek and five on her right.

"What brings you here, anyway?" she said.

"I'm helping a friend deliver something."

She looked around and over my shoulder. "And where is your friend?"

I turned and pointed down the hill towards town. "Back that way," I said.

She looked at me through narrowed eyes. "Right," she said, with a nod of the head.

"I'm serious."

Sophia smiled another big smile, then carried on up the hill.

"Do you like it here?" I asked.

"It's home," she replied. "But I'm leaving soon."

"Where are you going?"

"To teach someplace. I haven't worked out where exactly, but that's what I want to do."

"Can you not teach here?"

"I can," she said, "but I think everyone needs to live a little first, and learn a few things, before they can teach others. Right?"

I nodded. "I guess so."

"What about you?"

"I'm working things out," I said. "I got turned down for college."

"Oh, I'm sorry about that."

"Don't be," I said. "Actually, I'm realizing it was probably for the best."

"So you came *here* to work stuff out?"

"No," I replied. "I'm with a—"

"Friend . . . right . . . I forgot." Her smile was faint and impish as she cast a sideways glance at the knapsack on my back. "What do you like to do, Hugo?" she continued.

"I write," I said.

"What do you write about?"

"I'm not sure really, just whatever comes to mind."

"So what do you like to read?"

"All sorts," I said. "I'm reading *Robinson Crusoe* right now."

"So you like adventure stories?"

"I guess so."

"Then that's what you should write," she said, her eyes as big as blue saucers. She stopped outside a white-painted house with a weather vane on top, and there was an Old English Sheepdog spread-eagled on the porch in the shade.

I came beside her, and as she whistled, the dog ambled over to greet her, its tongue lolling from side to side.

"Hugo, meet Hugo," she said.

"I see the likeness now," I replied, as the dog nudged my hand with its dry nose. I petted him on the head and felt the knots of his straggly hair between my fingers.

"Thanks for your help," she said.

"No problem," I replied, as I put the grocery bags down on the porch. "It was nice to meet you."

"You too."

There was a tense silence, and I turned to leave, but got no further than ten steps before I turned back to face her. "Maybe we could do this again sometime?" I said.

She beamed. "I'd like that very much."

"I'll be busy for a few days so—"

"It's okay," she said, as she stood with a glint in her eye. "And good luck."

"What with?"

"Your *friend* . . ."

I rolled my eyes and smiled, and after we exchanged numbers we parted ways, and I strolled back down the hill towards the center of town.

Virgil was nowhere to be seen when I made it back to the main thoroughfare, so I returned to my spot under the giant cedar tree and closed my eyes as the sun settled on my face.

∽

It was dark when I woke again, and Virgil stood over me, kicking my foot. I rubbed my eyes and got to my feet. "You said you'd be an hour," I remarked, stretching my back.

"I saw you leave with the girl," he replied. "I thought you'd be longer."

"You've been following me?"

"No. I said I saw you leave."

"Where have you been all this time?"

"I told you, delivering something." Virgil stood there, empty-handed. He looked up at the moon that was sat like a snow-white disk against the black of the sky. "We should start heading back," he said. "We have a long journey ahead of us."

∽

We walked back the same way we came, past the craggy hills and into the dark pine forest with nothing but a lamp for light. A wind blew in from the north and down across the valley floor where it whipped up plumes of dust and dirt from the ground.

Virgil walked in silence, and so did I. And all I could think about was Sophia and her red tresses.

When we reached the foot of a steep cliff, Virgil stopped and said it would be a suitable spot to set up camp for the night. We emptied the contents of the knapsack and took shelter in a wide hollow that was etched into the rock face.

After we ate, I sat down to read my book by the camp fire whilst Virgil slumbered in the hollow, and through the crack and glow of the dying embers, I could hear the faded wails of ancient tribesmen brought down through the torrid wind above the high scarp. And, as I listened, paralyzed by the war cries of forgotten men, the voices spoke to me of wolves and darkness and death, like the words of prophets peering into the innermost parts of my soul.

My body shivered as the voices came and went, but I could not speak, only listen, silenced by the terrors of their whisperings. And as I sat in the still of the night, with beating heart, I remembered the dream I had had since I was a child.

In the dream I was alone, in the darkest of woods, and I could not see, only hear, as slavering wolves surrounded me from all sides, baring their fangs with raised hackles. There was no escape, and all I could do was wait, blinded by fear, as the wolves approached, ready to feast. And although I had never understood what the dream had meant, I was certain that my greatest challenge was yet to unfold.

CHAPTER 8

I awoke the next morning to the sound of birdsong in the trees, and Virgil was up and scattering seed on the ground. I squinted against the morning light and climbed down from the hollow in the rock face where I had napped, unable to tell if the voices in the wind that I had heard in the night, and the wolves and torments of which they spoke, had been nothing more than another dream.

As Virgil turned to face me, I had to look twice at the man who stood before me. The lines on his face had now almost vanished, and his beard looked fuller and darker than I remembered it yesterday. If it was possible, he looked as though he was growing more youthful with each waking day.

"Are you ready to head back?" he asked, stood with his hands behind his back. The timbres in his voice were also sharper to the ear.

"Yes," I said. "I'll gather my things."

As I packed my belongings into the knapsack, I realized that the pocket where I had stowed my notebook was empty. I searched the ground cover and path, but found nothing but dry earth and burned ash from the dead campfire, and, as I glanced up at Virgil, I spotted a flock of black-capped chickadees descend upon him to peck at the fallen seed at his feet. From where I stood, he appeared like a messiah amongst these gentle warblers as he lifted his arms in greeting.

"We all take from nature," he said, as the birds took wing again. "But what counts is what we give back."

I nodded, and he looked at my grave face as I stepped towards him.

"Is something the matter?" he asked.

"I've lost my notebook," I said, chewing my bottom lip in frustration.

"Where did you last have it?"

I recounted my steps from the day before and remembered that I had sat down to write under the giant cedar in the center of town, right before I had spotted Sophia coming out of the grocery store. "I must have left it under that tree back in Albion," I said. "I have to go back for it."

Virgil lifted his head with a deadpan expression. "It is a long way back," he said.

"I know, but it was a gift from my brother."

Virgil nodded in acceptance. "Then you must go."

∼

WE FOLLOWED the same route that we had taken the day before and Virgil accompanied me for part of the journey until we reached a small brook on the edge of the timberland before the main trail towards town.

Next to the water's edge was the trunk of a felled pine, and Virgil sat on it to watch the bobbing of fish on the surface. "I will wait here," he said, folding his arms across his chest. He didn't seem vexed or troubled, he just sat and watched, as if he were at peace with the world.

"I'm sorry," I said, "I will be back as soon as I can."

"There is no rush," he replied, as he turned back to the fish.

I came and sat beside him on the trunk. "Can you tell me what the next step is?" I said. "I can think on it during my walk to town."

He placed a hand on my shoulder and squeezed it tightly. "You have learned the importance of making decisions and taking action, but you must keep in mind that your actions should always be honorable," he said. "Do not sacrifice your honor for temptation or greed, or envy, or anything else. You must deal with people fairly because, to stand in another man's shoes, is to know what it is to be human."

"Okay," I said, "I understand."

"And remember this . . ." he continued. "No man is the master of another man's moral purpose. If you stand for honor, no one can truly harm you, because no person can ever take your integrity and justness."

∽

I LEFT Virgil by the water and continued the trail until I picked up the main highway to Albion.

From a distance, the town looked as though it was cloaked in a thick haze that hung about the tops of roofs and drifted further skywards. But as I drew closer, I could see that the haze was in fact smoke sent forth from a homestead on the border of the town, and there was the smell of a fire.

By the time I reached the homestead, the sky was painted in a red haze and the air was suffocating as I coughed to clear my lungs.

Outside stood a man and a woman, and beside her, a small boy no older than eight. The man was holding a length of pipe connected to a hydrant outside the main farmhouse, and he held the pipe with two hands and doused the blackened barn with water.

I watched from the roadside and turned to face the woman. Her eyes were wet with tears, and she led the boy by the hand and came towards me.

"Can I help at all?" I said, not knowing what else to say.

"Thank you," the woman said, "but it's too late."

"What happened?"

The woman stifled a sob and pulled the boy in close to her hip. "Harlan Jessop, that's what happened," she said.

I looked at her like someone to whom the name meant nothing.

"That man's the scourge of this town. I rue the day we ever took money from his hand," she said.

"This man did this to you?"

"No one else around here has it in them, or a reason to. This is how he likes to do business." She wiped her face with a handkerchief and glanced back over her shoulder to the ruined barn. She was weeping again when she turned back to face me. "There were things in there that belonged to my great-grandmother. Irreplaceable things."

"Why did he do this?"

"We borrowed some money and fell behind on a few payments. My husband's been sick, so I had to look after him, all the while keeping this place running and being a mother single-handedly," she said, running a hand over the top of the little boy's head. "It's not been easy. Business has been slower with my husband unable to work, and Jessop knows it. I told him he'd get his money, but he's a man without a mite of mercy."

I listened as the woman spoke, and looked down at the boy beside her, who hid his face behind the flounce of her dress.

"Everyone in this town is too darned scared to gainsay that man, so he walks around here with impunity."

From where I stood, I watched her husband lay down the length of pipe in surrender as the blaze took hold.

My blood boiled. These people did not deserve this. Anyone could tell they were decent, hard-working folk.

"How much do you owe?" I said. "If you don't mind my asking . . ."

"Five hundred, that's all. Just enough to see us by. I said we could pay him back when we were back up and running again," she said, as she heaved a sigh.

I took all the money from my pocket, which was no less than five hundred dollars, and held it out with an open palm.

The woman's eyes lit up and her cheeks reddened as she smiled a half-smile. "That's very sweet of you," she said. "But I cannot accept this." She took my hand in hers, then pulled back again. "We're meeting Mr. Jessop later at his bar in town to talk it out. But you are a kind boy, and I appreciate you stopping by."

The woman turned and wandered back over to her husband, who was lying flat on his back in the dirt now. And as she went, the young boy holding her hand turned his head to me and waved goodbye.

∽

I REACHED town a short time before noon. The day was as warm as the last, and the faces of the townsfolk glistened in the searing heat.

I checked for my notebook under the giant cedar where I had sat to write the day before, but there was no sign of it in the underbrush. And when I glanced up at the rows of shops that sat either side of the thoroughfare, I saw a hanging sign that said *Jessop's Bar* on the building on the corner of the block.

The place was near empty when I entered, except for two local barflies who had taken up their seats for the day. Their faces were ruddy, and they sipped on their cold beers and muttered something to one another. Something only legible to those who had liquor in them. They turned their heads as I walked over to a portly woman stood behind the bar, wolfing down a purple-berry ice pop. Her eyes narrowed as she saw me approach.

"Can I help you?" she said.

"Is this Harlan Jessop's place?" I said, looking about the bar.

"That's what the name on the door says, doesn't it?"

"Yes."

"Then I'd say you're in the right place."

"Is he here?"

She licked the remnants of the ice pop clean off the stick and then her lips. "What business do you have with Mr. Jessop might I ask?"

"It's about the family down the way there."

"Which folk are you talking about?"

"The one on the homestead with the barn."

There was a silence now.

"Uh huh," she said. "What about them?"

"I'd like talk to Mr. Jessop about the fire?"

She cackled and laughed from the pit of her fat belly and took a napkin from the bar to wipe her mouth dry. "Is that right?" she said, and her lungs wheezed as she spoke. "Well, he's not here."

"Can I ask when he will be back?"

The woman leaned across the bar and looked hard at me. "What have they been saying to you, anyway?"

Before I opened my mouth to speak again, I felt the warm breath and presence of someone behind me.

"Is there a problem here, Dolores?" came a voice, and it was close enough to send a shiver down my spine.

The man stood to my rear was hollow-cheeked and wore a plaid shirt over a tobacco-stained vest. As he took a drag on his cigarette, I counted three fingers and a thumb on his right hand, and there was a stump where his pinky used to be. He regarded me with a steely stare, and I could see that his teeth were yellow and crooked and he reeked of gasoline.

"He wants to speak to Harlan," said the woman.

The man with four fingers took another drag on his cigarette and puffed the smoke into my face. "Is that right?" he said. "And what does a kid like you want that concerns Mr. Jessop?"

"Says it's something to do with those Kindersley folk," the woman said, beating me to it.

The man drew up a wad of phlegm and spat into an empty glass on the bar. "Mr. Jessop's presently preoccupied. So, if there's something you want to say, I'll be sure to pass on any message . . ." he said.

There was a thud in my chest as if my heart were trying to punch its way out, but I held my nerve. "I'd like to speak to him directly," I said. "If it's all the same to you."

He raised a brow, then looked to his right as the door flew open and another man with greased-back hair walked in.

This man wore a white cotton shirt open at the chest and sported a thick mustache. He took off his sunglasses and kissed the woman behind the bar. "What's going on, Bill?" he said, turning to face the man with four fingers now, who licked his yellow-stained teeth and shrugged his shoulders in response.

"He wants to talk to you," he replied.

"Who does?"

"I do," I said.

Harlan Jessop was as tall as he was wide, and he flared his nostrils as he looked down at me. "Do I know you?" he said.

"No," I replied.

"Then what are you doing in my bar?"

"He said he's here about the Kindersley's," the woman said.

Jessop nodded and pinned me to the wall with a stare. "Is that so?"

I nodded.

"What about them?"

"He didn't say," the woman replied, coughing up her lungs again.

"I was talking to the kid," Jessop said. He turned back to face me again. "Did they ask you to come here?"

"No," I said, trying to steady my breaths. "But I saw what you did to their barn."

Jessop stepped forward and leaned into my ear. "Be careful, son." There was liquor on his breath and his face was perspiring.

"Maybe we can talk in private?" I said.

Jessop stretched his neck to one side and looked at his number two—the one he called Bill—stood beside him, who shrugged his shoulders for a second time.

"You've got two minutes," Jessop said.

I followed Jessop into the back office, and the man called Bill followed me, and I could feel the warmth of his breath on the nape of my neck as we went.

"It's fine, Bill," Jessop said, as he slumped down into a leather armchair. "I think I can handle it from here."

Bill looked me up and down and then closed the door on his way out.

I let my eyes wander the room for a moment, taking it in. There was a large vignetted landscape sketch tacked to the wall, and an assortment of snuffboxes lined up in a display cabinet. And atop the pile of papers on Jessop's desk, I caught sight of my notebook.

"Take a seat," he said, as he lit the half-smoked cigar that had been resting on the side of an ashtray.

The room was hot and sticky, and there was a lingering smell of stale tobacco in the air.

"I'll stand," I replied.

"Suit yourself," he said. "You're lucky I came when I did. Wild Bill's not as patient a man as I am, and there's a reason he's missing a finger . . . but that's a story for another time."

I drew in a breath and puffed out my chest. "They said they owe you money—"

"What's it to you?"

"I've come here to settle what's due. How much?"

He blew the cigar smoke out into a cloud and then sat forward in his chair. "Five-fifty, plus interest. Call it six hundred and we're square." he said.

I put a hand into my pocket, counted out six hundred in notes, then put it down on the desk in front. It was everything I had to my name. "That's six hundred there," I said.

Jessop's eyes narrowed as he crossed one leg over the other. "What is this?"

"It's what they owe you, plus interest. You can count it if you don't trust me."

He smiled a crooked smile and scratched his chin. "Who are you?"

"Just someone who doesn't want to see a family ruined over money."

"Is that so?" he said.

A silence hung in the air.

"They would have paid you back," I said. "They've just had a hard time."

"I know all about their woes," Jessop said. "But guess

what? The world doesn't stop for the Kindersley's, nor any other wretch that I know."

"I guess it doesn't," I said. As I tilted my head to one side, I noticed a framed picture of Jessop and the woman from the bar atop the mantelpiece. In the picture they stood, side by side and in better days, his arm around her waist. "Is that your wife?"

"Dolores? What about her?"

"If you had to choose between keeping this place going, or caring for your sick wife, what would you do?"

Jessop sat there with a vacant look and said nothing. "It's their problem, kid," he said. "Not mine."

"Not this time. But one day it might just be *your* problem. Everyone has their turn to roll the dice."

Jessop got to his feet with a clenched fist and said, "Is that a threat?"

His head was higher than the door frame from where I stood, but I didn't so much as flinch as he stepped towards me. "It's no threat," I said. "Just promise me you'll leave them alone."

"I don't take lectures from anyone in my own bar, especially from a pimple-nosed kid," he said, as he let out a breath. "But money is money, so let's call this one even."

I nodded and turned to leave. "One more thing . . ." I said, pointing to my notebook on the desk. "That belongs to me."

Jessop picked up the notebook and thumbed through it until a fold of paper fell from its pages: the map the traveler had left behind. He squatted to retrieve the map from the floor, opened it out in his hands, then looked up at me again. "This is yours?" he said.

"Yes," I replied, "and I'd like it back."

Jessop scanned the front and back. "Can't see your name on it."

"It's mine. I left it under that tree outside."

Jessop folded the map together again, slipped it back inside the notebook, and placed it back down on the desk amongst his papers. "I'll tell you what," he said, with a smug grin on his face. "You can have it. But I want something in return."

I held his gaze and said, "There's nothing I would do for you."

Jessop scowled and ran a finger through his oily hair, then glanced down at his wristwatch. "Then you can get the hell out of my bar, because your two minutes are up."

∽

BLACK CLOUDS HAD GATHERED in the east by the time I reached the outskirts of town again. I took the same route back and picked up the trail towards the pine forest as the clouds brought rain that fell to the earth like black tendrils.

I walked, soaked to my skin, back up through the dusty hills where the ground had now turned to silt and clay. I thought of Elijah and the notebook he had given to me and felt a sense of terrible guilt that I had had to leave it behind. But I realized now, that sometimes you had to be ready to let go of the things you cared about most.

Virgil was sat in the same place I had left him, and the rain had quelled to a fine spit by the time I had made it back to the brook.

"Did you find it?" he said.

"Yes," I replied, "but I had to leave it behind."

Virgil regarded me with a quizzical look.

"I'll explain it on the way back," I continued.

We walked back through the forests and up through the mountain passes, and I told Virgil of the Kindersley's homestead and the fire and Harlan Jessop, and he listened until I said all that I wanted to say.

"I sense anger in your voice," he remarked.

"Yes," I replied. "I am angry. What Jessop did to those people was undue."

"It is," he said. "And you may come across others in your own life who want nothing more than to see you fail, or do you harm. But even your foes are not worth your loathing."

"What do you mean?"

"Not everyone is as right-minded as you may be; not everyone will match up with your own moral compass. But even though you may have your foes, the best you can do is wish them well."

"Why?"

"Because if they were as kind and as honorable as you, they would no longer be your foe at all, but your friend."

As we climbed to the ridgeline, I could see more clouds coming in from the north, and they covered the last of the evening sun like the dusky veil of a grieving widow.

"Looks like a storm's coming in," I said.

"Yes," said Virgil, "we best get back before dark."

CHAPTER 9

We returned to the log cabin by nightfall and came inside, out of the bluster of the wild mountain wind. The trek back up had been harder than the one going down, and I kicked off my boots at the door and lolled in the chair as Virgil got a fire going in the hearth. Yet, despite my languidness, I was filled with a sense of triumph.

When we sat down for supper, I asked Virgil if he had heard the whispers of the tribesman in the night. He said that he had not, and I told him of my dream about wolves stalking me as I wandered blind through a forest.

"You have had this dream before?" he said.

"Yes," I replied, "many times."

"And what do you think it means?"

"I don't know. It's just a dream."

Virgil sat up and swallowed down a spoonful of beans and rice. "Do you want to know what I think?"

"Sure."

"I think it means that you lack the courage and conviction to face others who confront you, and the courage to face yourself without counsel. I think it means that your greatest fear is being alone in this world."

Virgil finished up the rest of his meal in silence, and I pushed the food around on my plate, unable to muster an appetite.

As he set down his spoon, Virgil wiped the corners of his mouth and looked up at me. "It seems like you have learned the value of integrity and honor today," he said. "Are you ready for the next lesson?"

I nodded.

"No matter how honorable our intentions or actions may be," he continued, "sometimes life disrupts our best-laid plans. Would you agree?"

I nodded again.

"We expect life to be a sail through calm waters," he said. "But a rogue wave will often steer us from our chosen course. Adversity is like a rogue wave. If you fight against it, you will end up but a sunken vessel at the bottom of the seabed. But, if you learn to weather these waves, and harness their power, then every new storm becomes easier to navigate."

"So the next lesson is about adversity?" I said.

"Yes," he said. "But, more importantly, how you master it. At some point you will suffer in life, like every other man that walks this earth. It is a part of the adventure of life. Things seldom go to plan. But to overcome your suffering, you must accept that you are not invulnerable to it, or deserving of its mercy. You must prepare for it always and confront it where you are able. Do not run from adversity, for it is the very thing that is sent to test our strength of character, our courage, and our self-discipline."

I frowned and sat back in my seat.

"You look unconvinced by this?" Virgil said.

"Are you saying that I need to search for hardship?" I replied.

Virgil smiled and shook his head. "The wise man does not go in search of hardship, but he expects it is only ever round the corner, and he prepares himself for it in times of ease and prosperity. The wise man does not seek to detach himself from the things that bring genuine goodness to his life for fear of suffering. He is free to immerse himself in his interests and friendships, but he does so knowing that, one day, like all else, they will come to pass, and the value that he has placed in such things will inevitably bring suffering when he no longer has them. The same goes for the people in his life.

"The cost of living a good life is hardship itself, but the wise man knows that such things cannot hurt his character, or the pursuit of his purpose in life. In the long run, it can only add to his growth and his knowledge—about himself, and about the world in which he walks. Amongst every hardship you endure there is a lesson to be learned."

I sighed and folded my arms across my chest. "I don't know if I can see it that way," I said. "How can there be a meaning to suffering?"

"That's what brings you here, is it not?" Virgil continued. "Because you are searching your soul. There is a suffering which you are trying to understand. You are trying to open your ears to its lesson. Is this not true?"

"I suppose it is."

"But you will not find meaning in your suffering because you cannot hear its message over the pain in your heart," he said, pushing his empty plate to one side.

"Then what *is* the meaning of our suffering?"

"Its message will be different for every person," Virgil continued. "But behind each tragedy, each misfortune, and each heartbreak, there is a common significance: they are all opportunities for us to learn about ourselves; an opportunity to build our resilience to worse things that may befall us."

"So suffering will strengthen me?"

"Yes, but only if you listen to its message. Remember that a warrior's sword is forged in a fire."

"My grandfather used to say that our struggles determine our successes in life," I said. "I think I understand what he meant by that now."

We sat there in silence for a moment, then Virgil got up to light a lamp.

"What happened to your grandfather?" he said.

"He passed away. A few years ago now."

"And you miss him?"

I nodded. "Every day."

"And you always will." Virgil rested the lamp on the table, and the flame cast long shadows across his face and across the walls.

"Do you think it ever gets easier?"

"I dare say it can," he said, lifting his head to remark my solemn stare. "Our minds must become like the warrior."

"How do you mean?"

"The warrior spends his entire life building his strength and mettle through hard work and fighting. It is the thing that will keep him alive. But even the warrior—the strongest and the fittest of men—still finds it hard to climb mountains. And our minds are no different. We have to endure hardship to strengthen our minds against future misfortunes that come our way.

"That does not mean you should not have emotion. In fact, it is quite the opposite. You should allow yourself to feel your emotions and own them wholeheartedly. But we can all learn to act with courage in spite of them. We can all learn to control them and stop *them* from controlling *us*." Virgil threw on his coat and took the lamp in one hand, and a gust of wind blew in as he opened the cabin door. "Come with me," he said, "I want to show you something. Bring nothing else with you."

As we walked out, I gazed up at the sky, and the stars shone and danced like scattered fireflies in a dark forest.

We trekked down once again, and Virgil led me to a small patch of land at the foot of the mountain where a strong wind swept over the open grasslands. And then we came to a towering maple tree that sat majestically under a full moon, and we stood beneath her like supplicants before a queen.

"You see this tree?" said Virgil, holding the lamp high above his head. "She too started life as a sapling. But as she grew, she was forced to plant her roots deeper and deeper to face the wind and the rain and the heat of the sun that set out to challenge her might. And now look how big and strong she stands."

We sat down on some rocks beside the tree and admired her beauty, and you could see that this tree wore the marks that chronicled a life of affliction, yet she was all the stronger and more enchanting for it.

"We all want for perfection in our lives," Virgil continued. "But perfection is an imperfect expectation. People are so preoccupied in trying to avoid pain and achieve success, that they cannot appreciate that their failures are the small steps that bring them closer to the very thing they wanted, because it takes time to master something that is truly worth mastering.

"So, instead of perfection, make tenacity your goal, because at the heart of every failure, lies the seed of another opportunity.

"To understand that suffering is a part of the rich tapestry of life is to release yourself from the fear of it. The sense of failure is nothing more than a collapse of your own—or other people's—expectations. You must keep your expectations in check because, if you succeed at this, then you will never fail, and you will never feel as though you have suffered, or have anything to fear."

Virgil placed the lamp on the sodden ground next to him and we listened to the sounds of the night for a while.

"I think you are right," I said, "I am afraid."

"I know," said Virgil, "I can see it in you. But now you understand that hardship is inevitable, and your fear of it is stopping you from living the life you could have. Is that what you want?"

"No."

"Then only *you* have the power to not let it stop you."

"How can I do that?"

Virgil reached a hand down into his coat pocket, withdrew a strip of black cloth, and extended his hand.

"You must start by confronting your fear," he said, placing the black cloth into the palm of my own outstretched hand. "Until you see that there is nothing to fear at all."

I held the black cloth out in front of me and looked at him, unsure of what to do with it.

"Put it over your eyes," he said. "Trust me."

I wrapped the cloth over my eyes like a blindfold and tied a knot at the back of my head, and the black of the night became blacker still.

"What's going on?" I said.

I felt Virgil drape a blanket over my shoulders and then I heard him stand.

"You remember the tribe that used to live in these mountains? The one whose voices you gave ear to in the night . . ."

"Yes."

"Well, legend has it that when a boy in that tribe reached a certain age, he had to undertake a certain ritual before he could be considered a man by his elders."

"What was it?"

"The boy's father would lead him out into the black of the night and blindfold him as he sat naked in the darkness. Before leaving his son to fend for himself, the father would then tell the boy to listen for wolves but, under no circumstances, should he remove the blindfold until the sun came up."

"I can't do that," I said, the fear setting in.

"Yes, you can," he said. "Trust yourself to see it through, and I will come back for you in the morning."

I listened to Virgil's footsteps fade into the distance and then I knew I was alone.

∽

I WAS BREATHING FAST, and I pulled the blanket tight over my body as I sat on the hard rocks, unable to summon the courage to move. Hours passed, but the darkness endured, and although my eyes felt heavy under the dampness of the cloth, I could not sleep.

Sometime later I heard the howling of wolves under a full moon, then a tug at my blanket as I listened to the sniffing of an animal at my feet. But I did not shout, and I did not move. And, eventually, the noises came to pass as the first cracks of light bled through the fissures of the cloth. As I felt the warmth of the sun on my face, I removed the blindfold and squinted until I could see again.

As I looked up, I spotted a figure sat before me, and then it rose and came forward.

"Good morning," said a familiar voice.

Virgil stood over me as I tossed the blanket to one side, his face cast in shadow.

"You've been here all this time, haven't you?" I said.

He smiled. "There is one part of the story I never told you," he said. "Even though the boy believed he was alone, his father had never really left his side. Yet he awoke this day as a man, having had the courage to face his fear."

I stood and stretched and rubbed my face.

"How are you?" Virgil asked.

"Tired," I replied.

"Like a warrior at the end of any great battle."

CHAPTER 10

We reached the plateau before daybreak, and the land to the east had taken on a new color as shadows from distant clouds roamed over peaks and mountaintops. And as the light touched his face, I noticed that the man I had learned to trust and admire was not the same man I had met several nights before, at least in appearance. Gone were the lines about his mouth that charted his years of doggedness, and his eyes had taken on a deeper shade of blue. In years, he looked at least fifteen younger than the night before, and there was no longer any sign of a hunch or a bend in his back as he walked. But I was unable to bring myself to say anything. It all seemed too unreal, like I had not yet woken from whatever surreal dream I was abiding.

Virgil sat me down at the edge of the bluff and looked out over the sweep of prairie below. "Last night you spent time with yourself and nothing but your thoughts," he said. "Before you commit to anything else, you must learn to be closer to yourself."

I looked at him with creased brows and kicked the ground

with the heel of my boot. "It's not like I can ever get away from myself," I said.

He turned to me with a flinty stare, his hands clasped together behind his back. "You will always be by yourself," he said. "But that does not mean you will like the person who looks back at you in the mirror."

"I suppose."

"You will always be alone in this world," he continued. "Yes, you have a family, and friends, and companions along the way, but you will always be alone on this journey of yours. Society will try hard to pair you up with a significant other, and you might marry and have children of your own to care for one day. But you must never lose sight of what makes you unique, because your uniqueness is your only footprint on this world.

"Never forget that *you* are the most important person in your life. You must learn to like yourself, love yourself even, and accept who you are before you can expect others to do the same in return.

"That does not mean you should be self-serving and self-obsessed. Rather, try to accept yourself and your differentness from others. Be genuine. Always be genuine."

Virgil reached down into the bag beside him and retrieved the tattered copy of *Robinson Crusoe*.

"Look inside," he said. "What do you see?"

"I don't know what you mean . . ." I said, flicking through the pages. "There are just *words*."

"Yes, but each of these words, when put together, form a complete picture: a story." Virgil lifted his head against the cool breeze and glanced down once again at the open prairie below as the first blots of cloud moved across the land like ocean groundswells. "Each of us has our own story to tell," he continued. "And every man is the playwright of his own adventure."

I followed his gaze and held my countenance against the breath of wind. "But I'm not sure my story will ever live up to other people's expectations."

"That's because you doubt yourself," he said. "I can see it in you, deep down in the shadows of your soul. Many people are the same, and it can take a long time to understand who you really are."

"Then how I can change that?"

"Your self-doubt comes from one of two places," he said. "First, from placing the opinions of others above your own. And second, from worrying too much about the past or the future."

I thought on that for a moment and then concluded that Virgil was right. I cared too much about what others thought of me, and I recalled many sleepless nights worrying about the things that lie ahead, and the mistakes I had made in the past.

Virgil placed a hand on my shoulder as I looked out on the darkened savannah, and forks of light pushed through the thick cover of cloud that hung over it.

"Sometimes we spend too much time living in our heads, that we miss the moment right in front of our eyes," he continued, as he led me up through a rough pass towards higher ground. "Our emotions tend to be fixed in the past or the future: regret is rooted in the past; anxiety is a fear of some future thing; sadness is for something lost; excitement is for something yet to come. And all these emotions are important, if only to remind us that the present moment is our most precious commodity. So, worry less about the past, and stop trying to predict the future. You will find yourself happier for it."

I turned to him and drew in a breath. "Then what's next?" I said.

"You are tired," Virgil said. "But I must continue."

"Where to?"

"I have something important to do. You can join me, or you can rest."

My eyes felt heavy in their sockets and my body begged for comfort. "What is it?" I asked.

Virgil turned off my stare and carried on up the steep pass. "Come with me if you want to find out," he said.

I watched him climb up through the narrow corridor towards a vaulting gray sky, and out to the west darker clouds had gathered, and streaks of lightning cut the sky like white barbs. And I caught the first spit of morning rain as it fell to my cheek, and with it came a thirst to follow. "I'm coming!" I said.

∽

VIRGIL STOOD WAITING for me at the top of the ridge.

"Wait for me!" I said, wiping the dirt from my rough hands on the back of my jeans.

We continued along the ridge flanked by needle-like caps and fractured rock shelves that bulged from the steep scarps, and to the south a flock of birds swooped downwind and across a mesa like a swarm of locusts descending upon a golden cornfield.

"Are you going to tell me where we're going?" I said, treading scree underfoot.

Virgil raised a hand and pointed further south to another ridge in the distance where a smattering of greenery gave way to a black cavern carved into the rock face. "There is an old artifact buried in that cave on the other side of this mountain," he said.

"What kind of artifact?"

"You will have to see it with your own eyes," he continued. "But it is precious and said to hold incredible powers to those who possess it. The greatest of powers."

I raised a brow in disbelief.

"It's true," he said. "You will see."

We walked on, up through a steeper pass where I noticed the black clouds from the west drawing in.

"What about the storm?" I said. "It's getting close."

"We weather it . . ." Virgil replied.

~

THE SPIT TURNED to a light fall, and rain was running off the end of my chin like a sluiceway. I wiped my damp hair away from my face and tried to focus on my footing as the path ahead became slick and cragged. And in the distance, the cave to the south had vanished behind a gray mist.

We hiked for an hour more, and the rain was falling in sheets and lashing our coats as I struggled to keep my hood over my head. With our backs pressed hard to the rock face, we tiptoed round the lip of a narrow pass that hugged the side of the mountain, and below us was a sheer drop to a bottomless gorge. And over the driving rain and twisting winds, I felt my feet slipping on the wet rock.

"Are you sure we will make it?" I said, shouting ahead to Virgil.

He squinted through the squall as he turned to face me, his beard sopping wet. "I hope so," he said.

I turned to see the land behind me, but the trail back looked more perilous than that which lie ahead, so we pressed on. And as we reached the other side, the path opened out onto a cliff ledge that sat high over a deep ravine, and further along was a decaying timber footbridge which joined the two sides of the mountain together. We stopped at the approach and watched the structure swing in the high wind. From the look of it, it hadn't been crossed for an age.

"We have to cross," Virgil said.

I shook my head and cleared the rain from my eyes. "It's too dangerous."

He inched forwards. "We *must* try."

Virgil placed a hand on the guardrail, held together by nothing more than threadbare rope, and pressed a foot onto the deck to steady it. He edged his way over the bridge, being careful not to rock it, and the structure bowed as he crossed the midpoint.

"Be careful!" I said, but my voice was only a whisper in the windstorm.

Virgil reached the other side and ushered me to follow with a wave of a hand, and the structure started to swing again as I reached out for the guardrail, just like he had done. As I moved across the deck, my feet slipped on the wet timber, and the ropes strained and teared as I grasped on to steady my footing. Virgil yelled, but his voice, like mine, was lost to the wind, and as I lifted my head, I glimpsed him through the murk, waving an arm across his body as if telling me to stop.

The bridge creaked and strained once more, and before I could open my mouth to speak, I felt my foot dangling in midair as the deck came loose from under me.

I gripped hard onto the guardrail to steady myself, and the structure sagged and groaned under my weight. And as the wooden deck beneath me cracked and fell into the blackness below, I rushed for the other side and reached out for Virgil's proffered hand as he heaved me up onto the greasy rock shelf as the ropes severed and the structure collapsed into the bottomless ravine.

I got to my feet, breathing hard, and Virgil stood at the

edge of the cliff, casting an eye across the chasm where the bridge once hung.

"How are we going to get back?" I said, my eyes burning into the back of his head.

"There are other ways," he said, as he turned and walked up a steep rise towards yet higher ground.

We walked in silence until we reached the cave on the other side of the mountain, past a line of spires and sawtooth peaks which surrounded it. The cave was etched into the side of the mountain like a hidden grotto, and we took shelter inside. It was dark and airless, and I heard my breaths repeat through the void. We sat by the cave entrance and watched the rain as Virgil lit a lamp for light.

"I could have died out there . . ." I said.

"But you didn't," Virgil said, with a smile on his face.

My hands trembled, and my skin was raw from the wind and lashing rain. "I'm serious. It's not funny."

"Every night you shut your eyes could be your last," he said, walking back out to regard the land below. "And every day you open them could be the same. To realize this is to appreciate that the temporariness of life is the very thing that makes it worth living. It's what makes the present moment so special. So, enjoy this moment, because you are still here to complain about it."

I stood and walked over to the cliff edge, then looked far south where the peaks and pinnacles touched the sky.

"Shall we continue?" he said.

"Okay," I replied.

Virgil led the way as we trekked further into the cave, carrying the lamp in one hand to light the path for us. And the wind followed us through deeper passageways as if it were the whimpered voice of the mountain itself. "It's just down here," he said.

We turned through another narrow passage and under a

low-hanging arch, and Virgil set down the lamp on the floor. He squatted in the orange glow before a pile of smaller rocks stacked on top of each other at the back of the cave wall.

"Help me with these," he said, as he began removing the stones one at a time.

I stooped to one knee and helped him move the rocks to a new pile beside us until a small nook appeared in the cave wall. And when we had removed all the stones, there was a flash of silver in the lamplight, and a small chest took shape in the dark hollow before me.

Virgil reached in and retrieved the chest, then set it down in front of me. "Look inside," he said.

The chest was coal black and had a silver-rimmed lid, and its surface was smooth and untarnished. I lifted the lid, and Virgil held the lamp high above our heads.

Inside was a thin silver rod, set in a black inlay. The rod itself was pointed at one end and had a rounded base.

"What is it?" I said, as I removed it from its inlay and let it roll in the palms of my hands.

"It is known as the Candle of Life," Virgil replied, looking at it with wonder in his eyes.

"What does it do?"

"When the sun is down, you blow on the wick . . ."

"And then what?"

There was a long pause.

"I do not know," he said. "But some say it holds the power of prophecy."

I took the candle in one hand now and held it out in front of me. "It can tell me my future?"

"Some say so."

"And you believe it holds this power?"

Virgil smiled in the lamplight. "It is a legend, that is all I know."

I glared at him. "You made me risk my life for this candle .

. ." I said, holding it out in front of me, "and you don't know if it even works?"

"You could put it that way," he replied.

"But why?"

"People have killed and have died for this candle since time began, regardless of whether the legend is true. People have pursued it without knowing whether their quest was ever worth it."

I sat back against the rock and thought to myself. "Life comes with no guarantees . . ." I said.

Virgil nodded. "Which is why you must enjoy the journey, and never the outcome," he said. "It does not matter if the candle has powers or not, if the journey alone makes it worth striving for."

"How did you know where it would be?"

"Because we often find the brightest of things in the darkest of places."

We walked back to the cave entrance and looked out onto a sunless sky. Rain was falling to the west still, and the night would soon be upon us.

"It's getting dark," I said.

"We can rest here tonight," Virgil replied. "We have food, and we can take shelter in the cave."

∼

WE ATE cornbread and tinned beans by the lamplight as darkness fell over the mountain, and we rationed the flask of water to make sure it would last us until morning.

The wind and the rain continued into the night, and I laid on my back in a restless reverie, unable to sleep once more.

Virgil slept on his side, facing the wall, as still and as silent as always. The wind brought in the cold, and I tossed and turned and pulled my threadbare blanket over my head and willed myself to sleep, but my eyes would not surrender to tiredness.

After a while, I got to my feet again, keeping the blanket over my shoulders as I opened the chest by the dying flame of the lamplight. Virgil did not move.

As I laid eyes upon the candle, I noticed that it was no longer silver, but black, and as I reached in to hold it, small white flecks emerged on its obsidian surface like a constellation of stars amongst the black blanket of the cosmos. And the white flecks shimmered and died as new ones took their place, and I could now see the universe before my eyes, twisting and turning in all its beauty.

I held the candle to my lips and blew, and the cave became flooded with the whitest of light, and the candle blinded me as it glowed in my hand. There was nothing but white all around me, and I called out for Virgil but my cries went unanswered, and I was running on an endless ocean of light, calling his name and searching, yet still there was no response. And then the light turned to dark, and I was drifting at the edge of space, with burning stars and spiraling galaxies everywhere I turned.

Then a voice came from the depths of the darkness, as if it were the voice of God speaking to me. "Hugo . . ." the voice said, and it was a voice I had heard long ago.

"Grandpa?" I said.

"I'm right here," the voice replied, as if resounding through a dark abyss.

I turned to see the face of my grandfather behind me—a face I could now only muster from memories of yore. "Grandpa . . ."

"How are you, Son?" he said.

"Am I dead?" I replied.

"No," my grandfather replied, "quite the opposite."

"What's going on?"

"You blew on the candle."

"What does it mean?"

"It means I must show you something . . ." My grandfather stepped towards me and held out his hand.

I took his hand in mine, and, as I did, the black of space was transformed into a green meadow, and I was standing among a field of wildflowers under a golden sky. "Where are we?" I said.

"We are standing in the place where your parents fell in love," he said. "Look over there . . ."

He pointed to a hill in the distance where a red oak tree stood tall at its center. As I watched, I glimpsed two figures emerge over the crest of the hill: it was my mother and father before I remembered them. They looked happy and smiled and laughed as they sat down next to the oak tree as my father played his guitar for my mother.

Then I heard my mother's voice, calling my name, and as I turned, I found myself standing in a hospital room. My mother was in the bed—some years older than in the vision before—and cradling a baby as my father cradled her.

"This is the day you were born," my grandfather said as he stood next to me. But my parents could not hear him, or see us, and we stood like invisible bystanders to a forgotten time.

My mother was crying, and my father was too, and they sat in silence and kissed one another.

I looked at my grandfather and smiled, and as I turned back again, my parents were gone, and I was now looking at my eleven-year-old-self sat at a desk on his first day of a new school. A girl with blond hair on the desk next to me—I remembered her face but could not recall her name—then looked at me and laughed. And then the entire class turned and laughed with her, and I could see, from where I stood now, that ink had blotted my mouth in a blue hue where I had chewed through the top of my pen. Even the teacher curbed a grin.

"Do you remember this day?" my grandfather said.

"How can I forget," I replied.

I watched my eleven-year-old-self rise from the desk, shamefaced, and run for the classroom door.

"I remember how upset you were that day," my grandfather continued.

I peered up at my grandfather again, who was smiling to himself, and I raised a smile of my own. "It wasn't funny at the time," I said.

My grandfather tapped me on the shoulder as he opened the classroom door, and we stepped out into a blinding flash as I covered my eyes with the back of my hand.

And when I opened them again, a new vision had taken its place, and we were standing outside a familiar church as a hearse crawled passed and slowed to a stop. Inside was my grandfather's casket, and everyone was dressed in funereal colors.

"This is when you died . . ." I said.

"Yes," he replied.

I watched my father and his brothers carry my grandfather's casket on their shoulders into the church.

I closed my eyes, unable to witness the echoes of buried memories, and when I dared open them for a second time, I was once again standing on an ocean of light, as if waiting at the gates of heaven itself.

"There are many memories like these which I can show you," my grandfather said. "But the past is the past, for better or worse, and that cannot change." He took me by the hand and led me towards two white doors which had appeared before us. "I have shown you your past," he continued. "But what does your future hold?"

I stood beside him, bereft of speech, and unable to determine if this was real or another horrid dream that I had not yet woken from.

"You have two doors in front of you," he said. "The door on your left will show you what your future holds."

"And the door on the right?" I said.

"That door takes you back to the place you came. But you will forever live your life in darkness. You will live blind like the rest of man, and you will always wonder what you would have done if only you took the other door."

I heaved a sigh, then let go of my grandfather's hand. "I don't want to see my future," I said.

"Why not?" my grandfather replied.

"Like you said, I cannot change my past. The only thing I can change is what happens now. Besides, it is the mystery of what lies ahead which makes the future worth living for."

My grandfather smiled and placed a hand on my shoulder. "I'm proud of you," he said. "Always was, and always will be."

As I went to move, I felt my legs give way from beneath me, and the white became black again, and I was sinking into an ocean below. I lifted my head and looked up, but my grandfather was gone, and I could see nothing but the ripples of water on the surface as my head went under. I thrashed my arms and legs, but I continued to sink, deeper and deeper, unable to swim, and drowning and gasping for air.

I choked for breath as I sunk deeper still, and as my foot touched the ocean seabed, I closed my eyes and let out a last breath.

CHAPTER 11

The dawning sky brought with it the sound of chickens, and as my eyes struggled open, I discovered I was stretched out on the straw bed in the barn. My head was thick and my body was stiff with cramp, and I stepped out and let the cool breeze of another morning touch my face as the first light of day broke through the mantle of cloud over the eastern skies. I searched the bluff, expecting to find Virgil stood to the sun in musing, but there was nothing but dust and rock.

The cabin too was empty, and Virgil was nowhere in sight, and there was nothing but cold ash in the hearth. I called his name, but was met with silence.

I could not remember the journey back from the cave. Had we even been to the cave? And what of the silver candle and the vision of my grandfather that had appeared before me?

Was *any* of it real?

I hunted for clues, and inside the cabin, atop the center table, I spotted a note which said that I should meet him by the fountain at the market in Meridian when I was ready. He would wait for me there.

I took an apple from the bowl on the table, threw on my coat, and headed down the mountain for Meridian.

∼

BY THE TIME I had reached the bottom, the sun had crested the peaks further to the east, and the air was thick with the scent of pine and juniper. I crossed the grasslands, damp with morning dew, and picked up the trail into town that corkscrewed through the shade of the forest as I listened to the chorus of birds in the trees.

The end of the trail stopped on the border of town, and I stood and listened to the distant din of voices and laughing. And, amongst it all, I could hear carnival music playing.

I followed the road into Meridian and crossed the cobbled paths to the main plaza. The market was astir, and the streets were alive with various traders and merchants and a bustling crowd to whom they peddled their wares. The entire town had turned out for the show.

In the main square, people shuffled around stalls and sideshows, and children played at a coconut shy and a tin can alley, and there was a carousel, festooned with a red and white canopy, for people to ride. And on the other side of town, families played in the warm waters of the selfsame lake as more locals had gathered to watch from the shore.

I edged my way through the crowd and the lure of the stall traders as they jostled for attention and spoke in tongues. The townsfolk were adorned in ornate costumes, cloaks, and carnival masks, and everyone was in high spirits as they talked and quipped over the marching sounds of a circus screamer.

I passed through a troop of stilt walkers and came to a

quiet corner where I could see a large bronze fountain set amongst a beautiful garden. It had a wide basin, and fresh water spouted from the mouth of an ancient, godlike statue that stood with a conch shell to his lips.

Couples sat in the shade of the pines with their picnics, and there was a cookout for the entire town beyond them. And under the shade of another tree, I spotted the figure of a man as he stood and watched like an unseen shadow. He wore a beard, and was no older than forty, but he stood with his hands behind his back just the same as Virgil. The strangest thing about him, however, was his likeness to me. In fact, I could have been looking into a mirror at my older self.

I approached the man in the shade of the tree, and he smiled at me. "Virgil . . ." I said. "Is that you?"

"It's a beautiful day," he replied, his eyes fixed to the crowds like a pilgrim before a shrine.

I studied him for a long moment, and saw more of myself than I had realized from a distance: his chin was the same, slightly pointed, as was the color of his russet hair, and his nose, like mine, was slightly flat at the end. It made no sense, but it was unmistakably him.

I went to speak, but was silenced as Virgil put a finger to his lips and turned me to face the crowd. I was too numb to resist.

"Look out there . . ." he said. "Isn't it beautiful?"

Townspeople were everywhere, making merry across the plaza and down through the narrow streets.

"It looks great," I said.

"There is nothing like the present moment."

His words hung in the air like the echoes of an erstwhile teacher, and it struck me with a sense of déjà vu.

"What happened yesterday?" I said.

"I thought we agreed not to worry about the past . . ."

"Yes," I said, turning to face him again. "But what happened in that cave?"

He fixed me with a stare. "What cave?"

"The cave you took me too. With the artifact. The candle."

Virgil shook his head as if he didn't know what I was talking about. "When we returned to the cabin from the night before last you were tired and weary," he said. "You slept all day and all night, and so I left you a note on the table in the hope you would wake this morning. And, well, here we are."

I took in a breath and rubbed my face. "But the cave . . ." I said, struggling for words. "And the storm . . ."

Virgil stood there with a vacant expression.

I looked down at my body, then up at the sky, and I pinched myself as if expecting to wake from this dream I was trapped in.

I closed my eyes for a long while and willed myself to wake, and as I opened them again, Virgil was still stood studying me with the same blank stare and through the same blue eyes. But he looked different now: his wispy beard was longer again; his hair was as gray as the mountain cloud, and the deep folds on his time-worn face had returned with a vengeance. He looked exactly like the first day I had met him at the top of the mountain.

"Are you okay?" he said.

I could not muster the words to respond.

He put a hand on my shoulder. "You have come far," he said. "You have learned much, and things may not appear as they seem. You're tired, but our time together is near its end."

There was a light in his eyes, and I stood there in silence.

"We must remain focused on the present moment. Do not use your mind. Do not think. The word *mind* means 'to think', so do not think," he said. "All you need to do is observe what's around you. Watch and only watch."

Virgil took me by the shoulders once again and turned me to face the surrounding spectacle.

"This is life," he said. "It is a festival to observe. A play. We are the actors on its stage. But we are also its spectators. And to focus on the present, you must not be an actor, but a spectator. To live a considered life is to take a step back and see the world for what it really is, because life is a show, and here are its performers . . ."

Virgil lifted a hand and pointed to the merchants and traders and the town's denizens, and they appeared to me just like he said: as performers on a stage.

"Look at these people," he continued. "You already know there are people in this world who live their lives for material gain; others for temptation and thrill, and even some for the drama it brings. But there are also those who understand the beauty of the spectacle alone. The observers of the world."

I followed Virgil's pointed finger to a girl sat alone on a bench, watching the festival crowds. And as I squinted to see, I recognized the red locks that tumbled down her face. "Sophia . . ." I said. "That's the girl I met the other day."

Virgil lifted his head and smiled. "A coincidence, some might say."

"Do you believe in fate?" I said.

"Do you?" he replied.

I pondered it for a moment. "I believe some things will always be a certain way."

We watched Sophia for a moment. Her face was long, and she folded her arms across one another.

"She looks sad," I said.

"So go to her."

I crossed the plaza, through the crowds of people, and slowed as I approached her. "Sophia?"

She glanced up and wiped her eyes. "Hugo?" she said, feigning a smile.

"Are you okay?"

After a moment, she let the smile go. "I've been better."

"What's wrong?"

"My grandma . . . she's sick." Her voice was breaking now.

"I'm sorry," I said, not knowing what else to say.

"She's not been well for a while. She's in a home here in Meridian."

I looked about the bustle of the surrounding market. "So why are you out here?"

"I needed some space," she said. "Just for a minute." She took in a long breath.

I sat beside her and said, "Do you want to talk about it?"

She hesitated for a moment. "My grandma doesn't remember me anymore. She doesn't remember much at all, actually. Not even my father."

"How are your family coping?"

"My father doesn't want to see her anymore. It's too hard for him."

"Are you here alone?"

"No, I came with my mother," she said. "She's speaking with the nurses, so I came out here to get some space."

I glanced up at the stir of the carnival again. "I think you came to the wrong place . . ."

She followed my gaze, taking in the hordes of people, and managed a smile this time. "You know what I mean," she said. "Do you ever look around and notice how everyone seems to go about their daily lives without a care in the world?"

"Sometimes."

"It's only when something hits you, we ever stop to think."

"I'm sure it's always been that way," I said. "And always will be. But I guess we never know what's going on behind the masks that people hide behind."

We looked out at all the people before us wearing masks, then turned to each other and laughed.

"You're right," she said. "And in some other town, in some other part of the world, someone is going through the same thing."

"That's how it goes," I replied. "But we can all find a meaning from our struggles. We all have the choice to act with courage in spite of them."

She held my stare and placed a hand on top of mine. "You sound just like my grandma."

My cheeks burned.

"Sorry," she said, letting go of my hand now. "All this talk about me and I nearly forgot to ask why you're here? Did you come for the carnival?"

"Uh . . . kind of," I said. "I'm actually here with—"

"A friend by any chance?" she said.

I peered over towards the pine tree on the other side of the plaza, but Virgil was no longer standing there. "He was there a minute ago . . ." I said, almost in protest.

"You're a funny guy, Hugo Driscoll," she said, shaking her head with a mock smile. "I'll be staying in town for another day, just to make sure everything is okay with my grandma. Will you be around?"

"Yeah, I'll be around."

"Okay," she said. "Maybe we can catch up tomorrow? If you're not too busy with your *friend* that is?"

She was mocking me, but I didn't care. "Same time? Same place?" I said.

"Perfect," she said, getting to her feet. "I'll see you then."

As she walked off, she shot a look back over her shoulder

and smiled her beautiful smile. "Do you believe in fate?" she asked.

I nodded, and she disappeared down a narrow street off the main plaza. I sat and watched the carnival for a moment, as a mime artist with a chalked face mimicked the crowd, much to their amusement.

"She will be fine," came a voice from behind me. Virgil perched himself in the empty spot where Sophia had sat only moments earlier.

"Where did you go?" I said.

"I've been here all along," he replied.

"You weren't over by that tree just a minute ago."

"Never mind that," he said. "How did you get on?"

"Her grandma's sick. She's pretty upset about it."

"That's understandable."

"I feel upset for her. It's not fair."

"Life is not fair or unfair. We are all indifferent in its eyes. Remember that."

"I know. I just can't help but feel sorry for her . . . and her family."

"Our emotions make us human. However, just like life itself, it is also healthy to take a step back and question our emotions from time to time. To rationalize them."

"That's a lot harder than it sounds," I said.

"It takes practice. Some may never achieve what is required because they will not allow themselves to take charge of their emotions. They view them as a separate creature to themselves because it gives them an excuse for their behavior.

"But, when we fall victim to our anxieties, fears, desires, or judgments, we must ask ourselves daily why they are here. We must try hard to look at our own situation objectively and rid ourselves of these negative impressions by questioning them. If the situation is not within our control, then there is little we can do other than choose the way we respond to it. The only thing that matters is one's ability to see what is beyond their control and choose their response with a rational mind."

"But how can we view grief with indifference? It goes against our nature."

"I am not saying you should not care. You should. However, just like you said to the girl, one can still be courageous despite one's grief. Your response to the things life throws at you is the only thing that matters.

"You already understand the importance of viewing anything outside your control with indifference. Well, that only happens with rational thought, and accepting the thing for what it really is. The same goes with every event in our lives. Our thoughts are just those: thoughts alone, and not the facts themselves. If every dreadful thing that happens to us in life is truly bad, then it would appear that way to everyone else. But people die, and people suffer, and it has always been that way. And not everyone will grieve for you, or with you even. It takes time to separate our emotions from events, but if you succeed, then you will be free from your pain. So yes, you *should* care, and care with all your heart. But try to question your emotions in times that call for it."

I shrugged my shoulders and sighed. "That seems like an impossible task."

"It isn't," Virgil said. "It may be the hardest thing you have to learn as a man, but when you feel like your emotions are getting the better of you, stop and ask yourself one question: what would the wise man do? Look at yourself as if you were one of these people at this carnival. Imagine yourself a bird looking down at the earth from a great height, seeing the world for what she really is. Because you will never be the only one struggling in life.

"Death—whilst the hardest thing you will face in your life

—will always be beyond your control. It will always catch up with you. But if you can learn to question your judgments, you will turn even your greatest tragedies into triumphs. This is really what separates the wise from the rest: being able to reason with your irrational thoughts."

"So rationality is the last step?" I said.

"There is one more," said Virgil. "Whilst rationality is one part of it, wisdom is also about awareness. The two must go hand in hand." He stood to leave.

"Where are we going?" I said.

"You will see."

I followed him back through the carousing carnival crowds, and, through a sea of masks, one man caught my eye in particular: he wore a horned goats mask with blackened eyes, and stood watching me from the corner of the road. He did not move. He just watched.

We continued across the main square, and out to a quieter street, and I thought about my grandfather and what Virgil had told me. His death had been the hardest thing I had faced in my life, but I could see now, despite the pain I held on to, it was always meant to be that way.

Only two days before he passed away, my grandfather had told me not to worry because he did not fear death. At the time I never understood how he could be so calm, but things were clearer now. My grandfather had lived a fulfilled life—he told me as much—and this was his reason for not fearing death. He had accomplished much, and he tackled his illness with courage like I had never known. And because he had lived a fulfilled life, he had no reason to fear death.

My grandfather was a lover of books, and I remember the last words that he ever said to me. He said that death was the last of life's great tests, like a writer finishing the last chapter of his novel. But, like a novel, it is life's last page which makes every story worth the struggle.

CHAPTER 12

"What are we doing here?" I said.

We stood at the bottom of the steps of Meridian Public Library, a large white building lined with tall pillars as if borrowed from an age-old Corinthian temple.

"This here is the keeper of stories, secrets, and knowledge," Virgil said, climbing the steps to the old oak door.

I followed him inside, crossing the marbled floor into the main lobby where thousands of books lined the walls two-storeys high. A row of desks sat on either side of the main walkway, and on the walls that had no books, hung the dusty frames of antique oil paintings.

I let my eyes drift over the room to take it all in. The library was empty of people, and you could hear the echo of our footfalls across the high ceilings.

"You have learned much on this journey," Virgil said. "You understand the importance of taking ownership of your judgments and actions and removing your self-entitlements. You understand that your purpose in life is to fulfill your potential in all your endeavors. You realize the importance of making decisions and exercising restraint to certain desires. You understand that taking action, and pursuing opportunities, is the only way to live a fulfilled life. Yet, you acknowledge that your actions must always be honorable, and that you should strive to deal with each person fairly. You accept the need to embrace adversity as your teacher. You understand that *you* are the most important person in your life. You appreciate that you must live for life's journey, in the present moment, and not for its outcomes. And you understand the importance of observing life's events with reason and rationality."

Virgil led me to a pedestal desk at the far end of the room and stood next to it. It smelled like old wood and was finished with green leather inserts and gold tooling on its top.

"But there is one last lesson," he said. "And all the lessons that have come before mean nothing without it."

"What is it?" I said.

"It is the last step of the path in finding meaning."

"Yes, what is it?"

Virgil pointed to the chair at the desk, and I sat myself down in it.

"It is *knowledge*," he said. "To let that go is to sell yourself short in every way. To postpone it is to resign yourself to a life of mindlessness; a victim of life's trappings.

"Wisdom is rationality, but it is also knowledge. And I do not mean mere intellect. This knowledge is sacred. It is not a knowledge of things or facts: it is an awareness of the self; the world in which you exist; the people you share it with, and your place within it.

"Knowledge is an awareness of the things that stop you from living a fulfilled and happy life. Everything you have learned leads you to this awareness and understanding."

"I know who I am," I said.

"I believe you do," said Virgil. "Some wrestle with their true nature for their entire lives. And others will pursue the things that only distract them from finding true fulfillment. You must keep this in mind always."

"So the last lesson is being aware of my true nature?"

"In part, yes," Virgil said. "The only sin in life is to be unaware. Do not be unaware, because the only knowledge that matters is the knowledge of oneself, and to know the limit of your own knowledge." Virgil stood in silence for a moment and pointed to the desk. "Put the key in."

"What key?" I replied. But, as soon as the words left my mouth, I realized what he meant. I reached into my pocket and pulled out the second key which he had entrusted to me on that first evening we had met on the mountain: the one with the silver stem and red jewel encrusted onto the bow. I pushed the key into the lock of the center drawer and turned.

∾

INSIDE WAS an enormous book with frayed pages made of parchment and it was bound in a plain, black-dyed calfskin. There was no lettering or embellishments on its cover; it was the oldest book I had ever seen. A tome of time itself.

"What is this?" I said.

"It is the Book of Wisdom," said Virgil.

The book creaked as I opened the cover, as if untouched for millennia. I leafed through page after page, but, as I turned, I noted that each one was as blank as the last. "There's nothing here," I said, tilting my head up at Virgil with a furrowed brow.

He smiled and said, "Why do you think that is?"

I considered it for a moment, then said, "Because wisdom is knowledge . . . and knowledge is without end."

Virgil smiled again, content with my response. "Which is why this book will always remain incomplete," he said.

"Throughout your life you will change, and your awareness changes with it. What you think you know about yourself one minute can change in an instant. *Change* is the only inevitability in life.

"Man's knowledge is often limited by his senses: what we see; what we taste; what we hear, and what we feel. But these are merely our means with which to experience the world; you will not know yourself through these senses. The knowledge I speak of is something different. It is sacred and unseen.

"We cannot see everything: we cannot see gravity; we cannot see atoms or air; we cannot see our minds; we cannot see emotion. But we accept that these unseen things still exist all the same.

"There are still so many things we do not yet understand about our own existence. But to understand *yourself* is to understand the limitations of your own knowledge. You will change, and because of that, you can only ever know yourself right now. And you can only ever make the changes you need to in the present moment."

Virgil leaned over me and closed the leather-bound cover, and I glanced back up at him.

"Because like every good story," he continued, "it always starts with the first page."

I opened the huge tome again to the first page, sat back in the chair, and stared down at the stark white in front of me. Everything that Virgil had taught me had led to this moment of awareness: this was *my* story to tell.

As I returned the book to its drawer, I heard footsteps on the marbled floor, and as I glanced up again, I spotted Virgil walking towards the entrance to the library with his back to me. And it was at this moment I knew I would never see him again. "Thank you!" I said.

Virgil reached the doorway and turned a last time, and as

we held each other's gaze, I was once again looking down the long hallway at my mirror image stood at the threshold looking back at me.

He smiled.

I smiled.

And then he left.

∽

I SAT STILL FOR A MOMENT, dazed and confused by it all, then got to my feet and hurried across the library, chasing Virgil's shadow as I went; past the walls of books as the soles of my shoes slewed on the marble floor. And then I glimpsed his shadow again, returning now, and a figure stepped in through the door.

But it was not Virgil.

His eyes were as black as coals behind the goat mask, and in his left hand he carried a gun: black, oily, evil. And as he lifted a finger to his pursed lips, I counted only three more on his right hand, and there was a stump where his pinky once stood. He lifted the mask over his head and came in and shut the library door behind him.

I stood there, unable to move, as if something were pulling me down towards the center of the earth. I recognized his face as the man from the bar: the one with four fingers that Jessop called Wild Bill.

"Where is it?" he said.

I shook my head and shrugged my shoulders.

"I won't ask again," he continued.

"I don't know what you mean . . ." I said.

He reached around to his back pocket and pulled out the folded map that the traveler had left behind. The map that had led me to Virgil. The map I had left with Jessop in my notebook.

He held it out in front of his face and stepped towards me, the gun still hanging at his side. "Don't be a fool," he said. "Tell me where it is . . ."

I said nothing.

"Where're you hiding it, kid?"

I swallowed dry.

He leveled the gun between my eyes. "I'm not messing with you, kid. Tell me!"

"Where what is?" I said, but it came out as a whimper.

"To whatever this map takes you too. That's why you're here, isn't it? You're looking for something. I'm not stupid. Gold. Jewels. Montezuma's goddamn treasure for all I know. Take me to it."

"There's no treasure," I said. "It's just a map."

He smiled a toothless smile and came another step towards me. "I know you've been looking for something. It's the real reason you turned up at the bar two days ago," he said. "Because you needed the map back. And we all know the only thing maps are good for."

"You're wrong."

"No. I've never been more right," he said, licking his bottom lip now. "Why else would you be poking around in here when everyone else is out there . . ."

"Have you been following me?"

"That doesn't matter."

I took a step back as he came towards me again. "It won't mean anything to you," I said.

"Mmm hmm . . ." he said. "We'll see about that."

"You're looking for the wrong thing. There's no treasure, or whatever you think it is." I turned to run, but Wild Bill grabbed me by the collar and pulled me towards him. And then I was looking down the black barrel of his gun.

"Stupid move," he said, baring his teeth. "What else are you hiding?"

He patted me down and noticed the hard ridge of an object over my pocket.

"Take it out," he said. "Slowly."

I reached a hand into my pocket and withdrew the silver key with the red jewel.

He regarded it with wide eyes. "Anything else?"

I shook my head, and Wild Bill swung his arm in a wide arch, and I felt a dull thud to the side of my temple as the butt of his pistol struck my skull. My legs buckled, and I collapsed on my back on the marbled floor, looking up at Wild Bill as his blurred silhouette stood over me. I pressed a palm to my temple, which was wet to the touch, and as I pulled it away again, it was streaked with blood.

"Get up!" he said.

I struggled to my feet as the nausea hit me.

"You're going to take me there," he said, holding the barrel of the gun level at my face again.

"I already told you, it's not what you think."

"Enough! Move!" he said, as he placed the map back into his jean pocket.

Wild Bill pressed the gun to the back of my skull, and I walked out of the library, wiping the blood from my face on the back of my sleeve.

∼

THE TOWNSFOLK WERE GATHERING in the main plaza as Wild Bill led me to his pickup truck parked on the side of the road, and I could feel his pistol pressed hard into the base of my spine to maintain the pace. A strong wind had blown in from the north, and as we reached Wild Bill's truck, he nudged me forward with the barrel.

"Get in," he said.

I opened the passenger door and lifted a leg onto the

footboard, and, as I went to climb inside, I noticed a flash of blue lights approaching in the distance and three police cruisers kicking up a billow of dust behind them.

The cruisers skidded to a stop a hundred yards in front of us, pulling across the road like a blockade. Five officers jumped out and hunkered down behind their doors, guns raised and taking aim at Wild Bill over the hoods of their cars before he had time to react.

"Let the boy go, Bill," said one officer.

Wild Bill glanced up, all weapons trained on him now.

"Put the gun down," the officer said. "I won't ask again."

"You've got the wrong man," Wild Bill replied.

"There's a warrant out for your arrest, Bill," the officer said. "Let the kid go."

"I ain't going anywhere," Wild Bill said, as he wrapped his skinny arm around my throat and yanked me off the footboard.

"Don't be stupid now!" the officer said.

The sounds of music had stopped, and all you could hear was the whip of the wind across the buildings.

"I already told you, I ain't going anywhere with you," Wild Bill said, tightening his grip around my neck as he held the gun to my head.

I tucked my chin into my chest as far as I could to stop the choking and, from the corner of my eye, I spotted the map hanging out of Wild Bill's right pocket.

People had started to gather now, and there were hundreds of eyes watching us, like witnesses to a Mexican standoff. Wild Bill looked around again. There was no way out of this for him.

"Let him go!" the officer repeated.

Wild Bill was puffing hard. He pulled me close again and started backing up down the street when . . .

Wa-boom! The sound of gunshot split the air, and everyone squatted for cover.

Wild Bill pulled back at the noise and tripped, pulling me to the ground with him. The gun fell from his hand and rolled underneath the pickup truck. He scrambled to sit, resting his back against the front of his truck and checked himself for wounds.

Wa-boom! Wa-boom! Two more shots rang out, and everyone squatted again.

I rolled onto my knees, then onto my feet, and brushed off the dirt from my shirt. And as I looked up, I glimpsed a stream of colors drifting to the ground: blues, yellows, reds, and greens. And then the entire street was blanketed in a harlequin sea of smoke.

~

THE GUNSHOTS HAD NOT BEEN gunshots at all, but the explosion of the huge carnival cannons and fireworks, timed to go off as the town clock struck midday. And the fireworks continued, exploding in beautiful trains of colored smoke.

"Get over here, kid," said the officer, coming out from behind the cover of the cruiser. He kept his sidearm trained on Wild Bill, who was now getting to his feet again, and still checking his body as though they had shot him.

I hurried over to one side where two more officers had appeared from another cruiser.

The lead officer stepped into the road and stood for a moment. "Don't make this harder than it needs to be, Bill."

Wild Bill said nothing for a long moment, then lifted his hands above his head with a sideways smile. "Sure," he said. "I don't need the kid. I got all I need for now."

The officers cuffed him on the ground, then escorted him to the back of the waiting cruiser and sat him inside.

He eyeballed me behind the closed window and smiled his toothless smile.

And I smiled back, holding up the map which I had slipped from his pocket during the scrimmage.

His smile faded to a grimace as the cruiser took off, back down the dirt road from which it came.

Everything was silent for a moment, and the crowds dissipated, turning back to watch the display. But as the officer approached me to talk, I saw one face amongst the crowd that had remained. Her blue eyes as wide as saucers.

Sophia.

CHAPTER 13

I finished giving a statement to the officer as the last light of day pushed its way through the blinds of the interview room.

The officer switched off the tape machine and put his pen down on the table in front. "Will you be ok?" he asked.

"I'll be fine," I replied.

"Where are you staying?"

"With a friend."

"The girl?"

"Uh . . . no. Another friend."

"Can I give you a ride there?"

I shook my head and said the first thing that came to me. "I like to walk," I said. "It helps me think."

The officer tipped his head forward and massaged the back of his neck. "Well, I believe that's everything. For now, at least. I may need to contact you in the next few days," he said. "For evidence gathering and all. Is that okay with you?"

I nodded and said, "Sure."

He slid the phone across the table towards me. "I can't

make you," he said, "but you ought to contact somebody yourself. Have you got family here?"

"Not here."

"Even more of a reason to call them. Let them know you're doing fine." The officer got to his feet and left the room.

I peered down at the phone, picked up the receiver, and dialed home. It rang a few times.

"Hello?" came a voice at the other end. It was Elijah.

"Hi, it's me," I said.

"Oh, hey," he said. "Mom and Dad are mad at you for leaving like that."

"I know," I said—it was as I had expected. "I'm just calling to say I'm okay. I'll be home in a few days."

"You want to speak to Mom?"

"No," I replied. "Can you just let them know that . . . I'm safe."

There was a silence.

"Okay," he said. "You sound different . . ."

I smiled to myself. "Just pass on the message."

"Okay."

"I love you, El," I said.

There was a pause. "Love you, too," he replied.

~

I STEPPED out onto the station forecourt and felt the warmth of the sun on my face. The officer walked me to the roadside.

"Are you sure I can't give you a ride?" he said.

"Thanks," I said. "But I'll be fine."

The station house was a small brick building on the border of town, with nothing else but open prairie land in every direction.

I started down the highway and walked towards the sun

that was sinking in the west and followed the main trail off the highway as I passed the sign for Meridian. From there I picked up the dirt track towards the mountain. Buzzards circled overhead, and I could see white smoke rising over the town as I neared the top of the ridge.

As I trekked up through the trails and past rocky outcrops, I thought about Wild Bill, holed up in a dank and sunless cell. I checked the map in my pocket and followed the trail to the ridgeline.

I was breathing hard by the time I reached the head of the bluff, and I could see a pair of yellow eyes watching me from the top of a rock ledge as I neared the small path that opened out onto the flat ground where I would find the log cabin. The eyes belonged to a golden eagle—and perhaps the same one that had greeted me on that first day. The raptor turned on its branch, ruffled its feathers, and took wing as I passed. I stood for a moment and watched the bird soar across the blood-orange sky, then disappear beyond the range further south.

I could see the cabin and barn in the distance, but there was no sign of Virgil, nor the chickens, and there was no scent of firewood in the air.

As I drew closer, I noticed that the cabin and barn were lying in ruins, like the forgotten remains of a forsaken land. The cabin was empty inside, and it smelled of rotting wood and animal mess, and empty cans of meat were scattered about the place. The barn was much the same.

No one had been here in a lifetime, that was for certain, except maybe the odd rambler who had used the damp straw in the barn as a bed for the night. And next to it, I found my rucksack and belongings as though they had never moved.

I sat down on the straw bed and pondered for a long while. The sun was setting across the range to the west, and the last hour of daylight was upon me, so I took shelter in the barn and decided I would leave in the morning. Perhaps Virgil would return, but my heart told me otherwise.

∾

I DIDN'T SLEEP that night. My mind was restless and racing, trying to grasp a way to explain everything. So I laid awake and listened to the sound of the wind and the footfalls of four-legged beasts.

I stayed until sunup, then headed back down and washed my face in a clear stream on the edge of the pine forest. The water was ice cold, and I smiled as I looked down at my bedraggled reflection on the surface, because it was the first time I had looked at myself in this way; in a light I had not seen before.

After that I followed the main road back into Meridian, its streets now empty of people, and all signs of the carnival from the day before had vanished.

I walked the quiet streets into the main square and sat on the edge of the fountain and read my book whilst I waited for Sophia.

∾

SOMETIME LATER I heard her voice behind me.

"I wasn't sure if you'd come," she said, as she sat on the fountain beside me.

"Here I am," I replied.

She was carrying two milkshakes. "I guessed you were a vanilla type," she said, handing one to me.

"Thanks," I said. "You guessed right."

She smiled and said, "Can we go for a walk?"

We wandered the streets in the noonday sun and talked

about everything and nothing. We talked for hours, and before long, the day had turned to evening again.

I told Sophia that I needed to head home for a few days and she walked me to the bus stop in the center of town where we waited for the last bus to arrive.

"So I guess this is it . . ." she said, as the bus pulled up.

"Only for a while," I replied.

She beamed, and I took the map out of my rucksack and handed it to her.

"What's this for?" she said.

"I wanted to give it to you," I replied. "It's the real reason I'm here. It's the reason I got to meet you."

"Because of a map?" she said, a brow raised.

"Not *just* a map," I said.

"It sure looks like a map to me," she said, flipping it over as if to find something else.

"Someone left it for me."

"Was this your *friend* by any chance?"

We shared a smile.

"No, someone else. But it's helped me," I said. "And I figured it could help you too."

She looked down at the map again, but with intrigue this time. "So where is this place?"

I pointed to the mountain behind her. "Just call me when you've finished."

"Finished what?" she said, a look of confusion on her face.

"Just follow the map, you'll see."

I kissed Sophia on the cheek, but this was not goodbye. I knew in my heart we would see each other again.

I showed my ticket to the driver and took a seat at the rear of the bus, and Sophia waited and waved me off as it pulled away.

I sat back and took in a deep breath, like it was the last

breath I may ever take, and watched the glow of the mountains in the twilight as we took the main highway out of town.

As my mind drifted, I thought of Jolie.

And I thought of Donny and the traveler.

I thought of Sarah.

I thought of my parents and Elijah.

I thought of the Kindersley's and Jessop and Wild Bill.

I thought of Sophia.

And as I reached a hand into my pocket, I took out the silver coin that Virgil had plucked from the stars that night on the mountain.

I smiled, let it tumble in my palm, and closed my eyes.

WHAT'S NEXT?

Thank you for reading *On a Distant Sun*. I hope you enjoyed it. If you did . . .

1. PLEASE SPREAD THE WORD

There is nothing more powerful than personal recommendations to people you know who would also enjoy the book.

2. WRITE A REVIEW

Your feedback is very important to me. An honest review of this book will help it reach the hands of other interested readers. If you are able to spend five minutes of your time **leaving a review** (it can be as short as you like), it goes a long way to helping me continue writing the stories you enjoy!

3. FOLLOW ME

Let's connect! You can follow me on:
BookBub
Goodreads
Amazon
to find out more about the books I'm reading.

Please read on for an Afterword about the novel and my hopes for the book.

AFTERWORD

There were two goals that I set out to achieve when I sat down to write this book. First, I wanted to tell a simple story. And second, behind the simple story, would be a deeper message.

By now you will have decided whether or not you identify with its message. Both are fine. But in both cases, I urge a commitment to open-mindedness. This book is not an enchiridion on life, nor does it contain any great secrets: it merely poses a question, provides an answer, and the rest is up to your interpretation and beliefs.

The lessons in this book are a set of philosophies I try hard to observe each day. They have helped me find a sense of purpose, meaning, and happiness in my own life.

The lessons of Virgil are not new, but borrow from both ancient and modern thinkers. Why? Because there is no universally accepted philosophy. If that were true, then philosophy itself would cease to exist, and the wisdoms of our great thinkers, both present and foregone, would be consigned to mere lore.

Philosophy is not a religion, and you are at liberty to

AFTERWORD

take parts to fit your own core convictions. This is what makes you unique. And to believe there is only one correct way of thinking, or living, or that yours alone is the right one, is both a haughty and flawed assumption.

Wisdom, in all schools of thought, calls for rationality. But there is no rationality in saying that one philosophy is right above all others, because the idea collapses at its very core.

You will not read this book and, at the end, have all the tools to understand your own purpose in life. And why should you? Life doesn't work that way, because your purpose doesn't lie in any external thing or book—it comes from you, and you alone. But what this book does, I hope, is offer some food for thought. A way to challenge your mind and beliefs in favor of some other way of thinking.

The lessons in this book are not tenets either: they are mere observations on the human condition. Never should we resign our thoughts and actions to sets of rules. Never should we allow ourselves to become psychological slaves. Individuality is the key to self-awareness, and vice versa. But if there is one rule, it would be this: be free to think, because freedom of thought is to know true freedom.

Yet, despite this, there is something comforting in having a map to follow, just like Hugo, and I can only hope that the messages in this book provide just that.

So where should one start? Well, we can all start by asking ourselves what kind of person we want to be. We can all choose the path of fulfillment, and we are all free to fulfill our potential in each of the roles we undertake in life.

Hardship will always find us at some point. Our lives will entail suffering and not go as planned. But remember that adversity is our teacher, and it teaches us we are alive.

We must live for the goodness of our being, and not for external pleasures and material gain.

Commit to action, because action breeds motivation.

AFTERWORD

If you believe in fate, then accept that fate happens *because* of your actions, not regardless of them. It's a chain of causality.

Finally, we must accept that our judgments and our actions are the only thing we can control. Life will throw all sorts at us during our lifetime, it is expected, but how we choose to respond is the only thing that matters.

R.C. Cunningham

ACKNOWLEDGMENTS

I owe a great deal to those who have guided me in my own path in life, and whose teachings and work continue to inspire generations, even after their departure from this world: Epictetus, Seneca, Marcus Aurelius, Lao Tzu, Siddhartha Gautama, Albert Einstein, James Allen, Viktor Frankl, Jean-Paul Sartre, Friedrich Nietzsche, Ernest Hemingway, Daniel Defoe, Herman Melville, Aldous Huxley, Ray Bradbury, George Orwell, and to every other person who dared to think and write about it.

Above all, I would like to thank the person who kept me going during the days of despair, and who gave me all the support I could ever ask for: Abbie.

ABOUT THE AUTHOR

R.C. Cunningham is a writer, poet, and lifelong muser. His debut novel, *On a Distant Sun*, was inspired from his interests in western and eastern philosophies. He believes that wisdom and inspiration should be shared widely, and enjoys hearing from readers who have their own stories to tell. He lives on the south coast of England.

> Follow him on BookBub and Goodreads
> Find out more on Amazon

Printed in Poland
by Amazon Fulfillment
Poland Sp. z o.o., Wrocław